monsoonbooks

SINGAPORE BLACK

William L. Gibson is a writer, educator and occasional sound artist based in Southeast Asia. His fiction and nonfiction work has appeared in magazines such as *Signal to Noise, Black Scat Review* and many others. His regular column on Asian art and media, 'Opium Traces', can be found at *popmatters.com*.

The album *Chillout*, by Gibson's experimental music project Third World Skull Candy, is available on BitPulse Records.

Singapore Black, the first in a trilogy of hard-boiled crime novels set in the rough-and-tumble frontier of 1890s Malaya, is followed by *Singapore Yellow* and *Singapore Red*.

Learn more about the author at: *www.williamlgibson.com*.

T0154783

Also by William L. Gibson

TRANSLATIONS
In the Land of Pagodas by Alfred Raquez
(with Paul Bruthiaux)

NONFICTION
Art and Money in the Writing of Tobias Smollett

FICTION
Singapore Black
Singapore Yellow
Singapore Red

SINGAPORE BLACK

WILLIAM L. GIBSON

monsoon

monsoonbooks

First published in 2013
by Monsoon Books Ltd
No.1 Duke of Windsor Suite, Burrough Court,
Burrough on the Hill, Leics. LE14 2QS, UK
www.monsoonbooks.co.uk

This second edition published in 2017.

ISBN (paperback): 978-981-4423-40-3
ISBN (ebook): 978-981-4423-41-0

Copyright©William L. Gibson, 2013
The moral right of the author has been asserted.

All rights reserved. No part of this publication may be reproduced,
stored in a retrieval system, or transmitted, in any form or by any means
without the prior written permission of the publisher, nor be otherwise
circulated in any form of binding or cover other than that in which it is
published and without a similar condition being imposed on the subse-
quent purchaser.

Cover design by Cover Kitchen.
Frontcover photograph of Battery Road, Singapore (1905) kindly
supplied by Antiques of the Orient, Singapore (www.aoto.com.sg).

A cataloguing-in-publication data record is available from the
National Library Board, Singapore

Printed in Great Britain by Clays Ltd, St Ives plc
19 18 17   2 3

When the nymphs heard this uttered by the Muni, they endeavoured to appease him; and they so far succeeded, that he announced to them they should finally return to the sphere of the gods. It is in consequence, then, of the curse of the Muni Ashtávakra that these females, who were at first the wives of Kesava, have now fallen into the hands of the barbarians; and there is no occasion, Arjuna, for you to regret it in the least. Death is the doom of everyone who is born: fall is the end of exaltation: union terminates in separation: and growth tends but to decay.

The Vishnu Purana, Chap. XXXVIII. The Curse of the Apsaras

Contents

Angsana Blooming   11

J. Caramel, Dead American   25

Sailor Town to Battery Road   46

The Mother-Flower Kongsi   61

Panglima Prang   84

The Boustead Institute for Seamen   100

Stone Water   118

Welbore from the India Office   138

Geylang Interlude   156

Municipal Stews   168

The Sport of Kings   185

Tantric Night   200

Evil Winds   217

Changi Jetty   235

Hungry Ghosts   248

HISTORICAL NOTE   253

MORE BY WILLIAM L. GIBSON   256

CHAPTER I

Angsana Blooming

IT WAS TOWARDS the end of the northeast monsoon, the monsoon that sweeps dry winds across the Deccan Plateau and across the Bay of Bengal, driving ships into the crescent-shaped Strait of Malacca. Everyone in Singapore noted that the monsoon was drier than usual that year; they speculated that 1892 would be remembered as the driest year on record. It had not rained a single drop during the entire lunar New Year festivities of February.

But on that bright hot morning, of the last day of the lunar festivities, which marked the beginning of the year of the water dragon, the tops of the tall *angsana* trees in the forecourt of the Central Police Station on South Bridge Road were flowering for the first time that anyone could remember. Their crowns had burst into fulgid blooms of white and gold that would, by the day's end, cascade to the roadway and gather in small drifts. Within another day the lightly fragrant petals would wither and brown and be ground into the blood-coloured dirt of the laterite road, trod under foot and hoof, crushed under cartwheel. The residents and natives of the crown colony of Singapore knew they would have to wait several more years to witness this spectacle again.

In the Chinese quarter, it was considered auspicious for the blooms to appear on this day, although it was difficult to decipher what this phenomenon presaged. Flowers the colour of gold could indicate wealth. However, white, the colour of death, could indicate a difficult year ahead. With such indeterminacy in perception, most passers-by merely gaped at the spectacle, shrugged indifferently and then went about their business.

To the Europeans, who had shut their blinds against the daytime heat for the last weeks, the blooms offered cause to gaze out at the unusual display of tropical splendour and hope that it presaged the coming of rain, to cool the air and wash down the choking dust of the roads. In fact, it should be said that neither the Chinese nor the European populations had much experience with *angsana* trees which were relatively new arrivals in Singapore: fast growing as well as large crowned, they had been planted in an attempt to provide shade along the wide roads and around administrative buildings.

To the local Malay population, these trees were simply another indication of British presence, therefore something neither to be resented nor completely accepted but to be tolerated as yet another marvel of both the natural world and Allah's will –to them, there was not much difference between the two. The transitory blossoms were meant to be pleasing to the eyes; what more need you know?

There was one European in the Central Police Station, however, who had some prior experience with the *angsana* trees. That man was David Hawksworth, and now, midway through his life, he was somewhat surprised to find himself to be the Chief Detective Inspector of the Detective Branch of the Straits Settlements Police Force of Singapore, although given the fact that the entire geography of his life had been bounded by the Tropics of Cancer and Capricorn, the position he held was perhaps not at all surprising. From his office desk on the second floor of the Central Police Headquarters, he could see the blooms of the *angsana* without having to crane his neck out of the open window. He was tall – usually the tallest person in the room – and had always found it uncomfortable to fit into a shorter man's world. Now, however, he had grown slightly paunchy, the muscles of his arms a little flabby, as he was self-consciously aware. Yet his face remained sharply angled, the nose slightly aquiline, the eyes acute, so that in profile he resembled his namesake animal.

A knock came at his door shortly after nine in the morning. Detective Inspector Dunu Vidi Hevage Rizby, adjutant to the Chief Detective Inspector, then entered the room, just as he did every weekday.

A native of southern Ceylon, Rizby was fluent in Tamil, and although a devout Theravada Buddhist, he possessed some knowledge of Hindu cosmology, which he had acquired while training with the Ceylon Civil Service at Kandy. In 1882, he had been transferred to Singapore to assist in the administration of the reformed police force after a Colonial Office investigation had unearthed extensive corruption among European officers on the force, up to and including the Superintendent. The entire upper echelon had been forced out, and administrative experts from across the region had been brought in to restructure the

Singapore force.

When the Detective Branch had been reformed in 1884, he had been made a Detective, because of his fluency in Tamil and in order to have him train the Tamil detectives. Proving himself to be as exemplary a detective as he was an administrator, he quickly rose to the rank of Detective Inspector. When Hawksworth was promoted to Chief Detective Inspector, it was understood that Rizby was to serve as his right-hand man.

Without greeting the man, Hawksworth simply said, 'The *angsana* is blooming, Detective Inspector. What do you make of that?'

'It is very beautiful, sir.'

'It is indeed. But it shall not last. Have you seen *angsana* bloom before?'

Rizby cocked his head to one side, rubbing an ear lobe. 'No, sir, I do not believe that I have.'

'Well, have a good look at them before they drop.'

'Yes, sir,' Rizby said before walking to the window and gazing at the bees flitting peacefully among the yellow blossoms, above the noise of the traffic from the street below.

He glanced across the street at the imposing bulk of the Police Courts building. The two police buildings faced each other, flanking the main point of ingress and egress to the Chinese quarter and the New Harbour docks that lay beyond. This was no coincidence but a deliberate statement on behalf of the colonial authorities: it was the police who controlled the flow of goods and men in and out of the Chinese quarter. The two buildings formed an imperial gate where all who passed could be observed and verified.

Rizby watched as a shirtless Chinese, rail thin, ribs poking out from under his dark skin, a conical hat on his head and with battered sandals on his feet, sprightly navigated the hot street, dodging past fast-moving rickshaws and weaving amongst pedestrians. On his shoulders was balanced a length of bamboo, and hanging from its ends were rattan baskets that held loads of bricks.

He stepped away and faced the Chief Detective Inspector.

Hawksworth, the back of his shirt already soaked into a delta of sweat, was sipping from his first cup of coffee for the morning and still did not look up. He simply motioned to Rizby to take a seat opposite his desk. The Sinhalese man did so casually; the two men worked closely together and had developed a strange sort of friendship that was bonded and contained by work. They never socialised with each other, but on the job they usually acted as a seamless unit.

'So what is this morning's report, Detective Inspector?' Hawksworth asked, finally looking at his adjutant. 'Another plantation worker eaten by a tiger? More smuggled opium discovered in the hold of a tongkang by our diligent river patrolmen?'

Diminutive and extremely dark-skinned with sharp features, a small mouth and jet-black wavy hair, with eyes that were vermillion and striated like agate and with somewhat pointed ears that seemed too large for his head and had small tufts of soft black hair growing from them, Rizby's face looked much like a fox's. He radiated a fox's intelligence too, a trait matched by a cunning savagery.

'Yes, sir, both. And another.'

'Another?'

'A body, Chief Detective Inspector. Found this morning at dawn in Rochor Canal by a Kling washerwoman,' answered Rizby, using the word that referred to the people from the Tamil-speaking lands of southern Indian, around Madras. 'Kling' was in no way meant as a pejorative

The sound of a horse whinnying in the traces of a passing hackney carriage floated up from the street below.

'And was the deceased also a Kling?'

'No, sir. It is the body of a white man. Nude.'

Hawksworth emitted a low whistle. 'White, dead and nude.'

'All three, sir.'

'Any reports of missing white persons?'

'Only Mr. Brumby, sir. And as you know ...'

'Yes, we all know where Mr. Brumby must have gone when his wife reports him missing. No other missing persons? In that case, inspect the place where the body was discovered. It would be good to have an identification and nationality for the deceased before the end of the day. If he is one of ours, this will not be as much of a bother. Paperwork-wise, I mean, of course.'

'Of course, sir.'

'Where is the body now?'

'At the dead house at Sepoy Lines. The coroner already has custody of the body.'

'Take a detective along with you to Rochor. I believe Anaiz Majid is downstairs right now. I will start at the dead house. '

Death was a fact of life that Hawksworth had become acquainted with at a very young age. Orphaned as a toddler when both his parents – he was told – died of a fever during the voyage from Liverpool to Penang, he was placed in the care of the Jesuit brothers at St. Joseph's Orphanage; telegrams and letters were duly dispatched in an attempt to find a living relative – in England, it was assumed – but no one had come forth to claim the boy. He remained at St. Joseph's, a ward of the colonial authorities, and was given only two items from his parents' baggage: a framed silhouette profile portrait of each parent. These featureless images were all he knew of his family, and they had stayed with him his entire life.

The Brothers educated him well at St. Francis Xavier's Free School, teaching him English, geography, maths and history with a distinctly Catholic perspective. An Irish Brother had once given him a tattered copy of the book *Abridged Works of William Shakespeare, Being his Best Plays and Poems*, which Hawksworth read as often as he could, finding this exercise far more delightful than the grinding lessons he was subjected to. Apart from the framed silhouettes, the only other possession from his boyhood that he still had with him was that book.

When he was about twelve years old, he had been allowed to go unescorted beyond the gates of the Church of St. Francis Xavier compound for the first time. Intoxicated with the freedom and fascinated by the swelling, reeling life he experienced all around him, he had quickly figured out a way to sneak out at night. Thus his education bifurcated into the harsh drills and standing delivery of the classroom by day and into the risqué streets of Georgetown by night. While he had been learning *King Lear*, he had also learned to speak street Malay, and he learned how to fight, and he learned that men and women are different in more ways than the Brothers had led him to believe.

His first kiss had been with a giggling almond-eyed Malay girl, and it had happened behind her mother's vegetable stall. His first fight had been with a group of Teochew Chinese boys, who had taunted him about how tight his shorts were. He had been soundly thrashed, but his fighting spirit – and his tall height for his age –had impressed the boys, who had then adopted him as one of their own. The nights of his youth, spent petty thieving, groping girls and surviving bloody scrapes with rival boy gangs, would prove to be fruitful for his later career. When he had been caught sneaking back into the boys' dormitory one night with a pocketful of pilfered tobacco, the Brothers had called the police, who had given him a brutal grilling and punished him with a night in jail just to scare him. The next morning the Brothers had threatened him with expulsion – not merely from school but from the only home he had ever known.

He never strayed again.

With regard to his beliefs, once, later in life, when standing before an admission board, he would be asked what religion he practiced.

'I was raised and schooled by Jesuit Brothers in Penang, sir.'

'Ah, then you are a Catholic.'

Hawksworth had paused to consider before correcting his

interlocutor. 'Suffice it to say, sir, that I believe in the Almighty.'

When he matriculated, the colonial administration had given him a stark choice: to join the army or to train for the recently formed Straits Civil Service. He had chosen the latter; he had sat for the exam, had passed it only on his second attempt and had been sent to study in Singapore. The police force, he had been told, was short of European officers with knowledge of Malaya. He was trained in the arts of arrest and colonial law, report writing and filing.

Hawksworth had gotten promoted to the position of Chief Detective Inspector when the officer who had previously held that position, Simon Lambert, had fallen into a disused tiger trap and died. Given his rough upbringing in Georgetown and his familiarity with local customs and languages, Hawksworth had been an obvious choice for the post of top detective. Practically every street in Singapore was given multiple names – in English and Malay, and sometimes in different Chinese dialects as well – and anyone conducting an investigation, anyone tasked with detecting evidence of a crime, would need to be aware of this, would be required to understand that a Cantonese speaking about the *ta ma lo*, or 'Great Horse Way,' and a Tamil speaking about the *kalaipithi kadei sadakku*, or 'hawker's shop street,' were both referring to South Bridge Road. Understanding such oblique cultural nuances was second nature to Hawksworth.

The only time he left Malaya had been to undertake an ill-fated posting to Madras to train in the practice of modern plainclothes detecting. He had just been made a Detective Inspector then. Working out of uniform, in the British society of the Indian city, the boy from Georgetown had managed to embroil himself in a contretemps with a young woman, the headstrong second daughter of a prominent nabob. Caught *in flagrante delicto*, the girl on her knees before him, the scandal had threatened to sully not only the good name of the Straits Settlements Police Force but the family reputation of the nabob's daughter. Hawksworth was quickly and quietly recalled to Singapore, where he had been ordered to keep his head down and his nose clean. It was strictly intimated to him that the further he stayed from polite society, the better it was for everyone concerned: he was police, and that was his place in their world.

The scandal had suited Hawksworth and his position just fine. He had been rendered a pariah, yet would be able to penetrate, when necessary, any level of society. Within the narrow social confines of a small colonial town like Singapore, Hawksworth was now a free agent: he was with them, but not of them.

When he had assumed control of the Detective Branch, there had been nearly twenty men working under him. Hawksworth and his men were not liked by anyone – neither by the local populace nor by their fellow uniformed constables. The locals referred to them as *mata-mata*, the Malay word for 'eyes'. They were not to be trusted, the people had decided, and were thus made outcasts in their own communities. The uniformed squads, on the other hand, resented the apparent freedom of dress and movement of the detectives, who were allowed to work in plainclothes and could roam about as they willed as long as they were investigating a crime. To make things worse for their department, Hawksworth knew that many of the detectives were on the informal payroll of organised crime, supplementing their income with bribes from Chinese gangs or from European- or Kling businessmen, who wanted them to look the other way. However, there was a small force of men in the Detective Branch that he knew to be trustworthy and loyal, and he used these men for his own investigations. They came to be known as Hawksworth's men, the *burung helang* squad, derived from the Malay term for 'hawk'.

* * *

After he had eaten his breakfast at this desk and had drunk his usual three cups of strong coffee, black with no sugar – a habit he had picked up in his youth in Penang – the Chief Detective Inspector made his way to the street to hail a rickshaw to take him to the morgue. He could see that it was going to be another scorching afternoon and, judging by the cloudless sky, another dry day. It did not feel like it was about to rain either: that humidity left a different impression, heavy and steamy, and when the rain finally came, it cooled things down. The equatorial humidity of a dry day was enervating: it sucked moisture from the skin, sapped strength and stamina, and brewed the elements of the town together into a hostile mash. It was malevolent weather, and it drove some Europeans mad.

A clanging double-decked tram rumbled down the street, spewing steam and smoke, and after it had passed, from behind it, appeared the head of Sergeant Major Hardie Walker. He was crossing the street, heading towards Hawksworth.

'Good morning, Sergeant Major. Bloody hot.'

'Bloody hot every day, Chief Detective Inspector,' Walker said without a smile. He pulled off his topee, the cork helmet he wore on his head, and mopped off the sweat that had beaded his bald pate. 'We could use a bit of rain. Some precipitation to cool down the air. Lessen the general agitation of things.'

Walker's khaki uniform was sharply pressed, spotless except for the sweat darkening it in geometric shapes. He was considered a cross-grained man by his fellow police constables, and some of the younger ones were outright afraid of him; no one knew why he could be made cross so easily; perhaps he was simply created that way, most assumed. However, he and Hawksworth had a solid working relationship. Both men recognised, without articulating it, that they were different from most of the other Europeans – they were lifelong residents of the East, and in many ways outsiders of their own culture.

Walter was now just over fifty years of age. As a young recruit (it was rumoured that he was an unemployed mercenary in Shanghai) Walker had served in the Ever Victorious Army under Charles George Gordon at the end of the Taiping Rebellion, and during this time had discovered a profound bloodlust and a pronounced disdain for all things Oriental. Yet he never left the Orient, serving in the army in India and training Sikh regiments there, then moving to Singapore in 1883 to train the police rifle brigade. Nearing retirement and wishing to settle down, he had left the army and joined the Singapore Police Force. As far as anyone knew, he was a bachelor.

Walker was considered a crack shot by his men. When the disturbances broke out in Pahang in 1891, he had escorted the rifle brigade into the town of Kinta, and into the heart of the uprising. He had taken along with him the breech-loading lever-actuated Martini-Henry rifle that had recently been distributed to the colonial forces in Malaya.

'Beautiful rifle. It was like shooting duck,' he had said on his return to Singapore. He had claimed to be able to get off more than fifteen shots per minute with the new weapon. 'Could drop twenty of them brown buggers without having my fingers get sore. Head shots, mostly. An accurate, beautiful rifle the Martini-Henry is.'

Walker's tales of the Dyak trackers, the tribal head-hunters from Borneo he had taken with him to Kinta, had left the deepest impression on the Chief Detective Inspector. 'We would send them into the bush to scout for encampments. They would come out as silent as they went in – only coming out when they had the bloody heads tied by the hair to their belts, three of four of them dangling around their waists. Damned sight it was. No matter how many times we said we only wanted prisoners, they simply whacked off the heads. Women and children too!'

That morning, standing under the *angsana* blooms, both men were anxious to get on with their business. 'Have something that might interest you, Sergeant Major. A dead white man in Rochor Canal. Nude. I am on my way to the dead house now.'

'Rochor Canal is a funny enough place for a white man's corpse to be found floating. Nude? Do not care for the implications of that. Need detectives for such work. Indeed. Do let me know if you will need my assistance in your investigation. Must go now.' He added gruffly, as an after-thought, 'Good day, Chief

Detective Inspector.'

Hawksworth considered Walker's offer to assist in the investigation. When not sharp-shooting or training men, Sergeant Major Walker was known to be useful as muscle; he could intimidate even the most hardened of criminals; in fact, he often intimidated the same men who had asked him for assistance. There was a strain of the sadistic in the man, but Hawksworth saw the value in that.

CHAPTER II

J. Caramel, Dead American

THE NEW DEAD HOUSE at Sepoy Lines was considered advanced by the standards of the colonial East. It was deemed the most state-of-the-art mortuary between Bombay and Saigon, and was paid for by subscription. The colonial citizens of Singapore considered the quality of their dead house to be a reflection of their own moral standards, of their scientific competence and of their belief in justice and rationality. In contrast to the barbaric practices of the natives, their clanging gongs and bizarre dismemberments, the dead house of the Crown Colony of Singapore was meant to serve as a beacon of the civilised world. Or at least this reasoning was used to raise money from the populace. In reality, no one wanted to think about the mortuary any more than they wanted to think about the sewerage or the collection of night soil.

Hawksworth reckoned he visited the dead house an average of half-a-dozen times every month.

It was a short and dusty rickshaw ride from the Central Police Station, past Hong Lim Green, onto New Bridge Road, along the fetid stream that bordered the north end of the Chinese quarter, and round the curve of Pearl's Hill to the V-shaped intersection with Outram Road. The mortuary was on the grounds of the General Hospital, conveniently placed across from the execution grounds of Her Majesty's Service Criminal Jail, more commonly known as Outram Prison.

Hawksworth knew better than to tell the rickshaw puller, an emaciated shirtless Chinese, burnt nearly black by the pitiless sun and reeking of opium sweat, their actual destination: the man would have protested vehemently and demanded extra money if he knew he was taking Hawksworth to the dead house. The Chinese believed that the spirit lingered around corporeal remains – and often the place of death – before slowly dissipating away, like a fog. Often the rickshaw wallahs would take long detours, despite the extra exertion, just to avoid running past the mortuary.

Hawksworth asked that the puller drop him by the prison entrance. He then crossed the road, walking towards the squat building about a half-mile from the main hospital, located on the top of small rise where the air was believed to be more salubrious. The new dead house was situated on a smaller rise, facing the rolling grounds of the hospital, its back to an impromptu cricket pitch.

Hawksworth found the coroner in the examining room, standing between two bodies placed on granite slabs. The room was lit mainly by a skylight, angled so as to avoid the direct rays of the sun. It kept the room bright but insufferably hot, made it seem like a solarium. Electric fans had recently been installed; however, all they seemed to do was simply stir about the humid air, ruffling the hair on the corpses. Once the autopsy and inquest were complete, it was made sure that cadavers were wheeled away as quickly as possible: otherwise, they would simply broil in the steamy light of the examining room. Bodies in an advanced stage of decomposition stank so badly that the skylight had to be swung open to help vent the stench.

Dr. Robert Cowpar had taken over as the coroner after it had been decided that the Superintendent of Police should not be able to serve in that post. At the time, inquests required a volunteer jury, and the coroner would merely act as a rubber stamp on the death certificate.

The policemen who had previously served in that position not only had lacked medical knowledge but were also given to drink and bribery. Cowpar, an experienced medical man, had thus been brought in from Calcutta: he was to serve as coroner as well as inquest jury. His ruling on cause of death would bear the weight of both the medical establishment and the colonial authorities. Moreover, he fit neatly into the new building; he was another cog in the colony's modernisation process.

'Good morning, Chief Detective Inspector.'

'Good morning, Dr. Cowpar. You are looking well.'

The coroner chuckled, 'Yes, the Singapore diet is doing wonders for my constitution.'

As are our women, Hawksworth almost said aloud. It was well known that Cowpar was all but in a common-law marriage with his stout Chinese housekeeper, his amah. The housekeeper, along with his residence, was part of the compensation awarded to him by the colonial authorities. When he had arrived, no one was aware that Cowpar was a bachelor; it was assumed the doctor was a family man, so a female housekeeper had been arranged. However, the doctor, who always stank of death, the rank smell of rotten flesh, has soon become quite unwelcome in polite company, and thus the happenstance arrangement with the amah proved to be not entirely inconvenient for him. And now it was too late to make other arrangements anyway, so the coroner grew fatter and jollier by the year, basking in professional approbation while living the cloistered life of the well-fed married man.

When he had first come from India, Cowpar had been as thin as a rail, but in the few years he had spent in Singapore, he had become portly, his belly bulging beneath the rubber apron he wore in the examining room. His face was fat now, too, red from having port wine with breakfast and exertion in the sauna-like examining room. His spectacles were thick and reflected the sunbeams from the skylight so starkly that he often appeared to have two circles of radiant white embedded in his face where his eyes should be.

'I was informed that a body was recovered from Rochor Canal this morning – a white man.'

'Indeed, and here he is,' Cowpar gestured with sausage fingers to the corpse on the table next to him.

Hawksworth saw that the dead man was not merely white but was very white, the sort of white that only the affluent could maintain in the tropics; the sort of white that suggested near perpetual seclusion from the sun's blaze. His face was slightly browned, as were the backs of his hands, but his skin was otherwise white as alabaster, covered in the light downy hair typical of blonds. His skin was smooth, free of bruises, scars or marks. The muscles were toned; although relaxed in death, they still shone athletic under the white skin.

The face was handsome but frozen in the death mask of the drowned, as though the last thing he saw was both terrifying and hysterical beyond words.

'Have you completed the autopsy?'

'I have completed a preliminary autopsy, and I will proceed no further unless you request it.'

'What killed him?'

'You must mean "How did he die?". Quite simple– this man drowned.'

'Time of death?'

'I would estimate that the body was in the water for about six to eight hours. It was reported found,' Cowpar flipped through a notebook that swung from a clip near the corpse's feet. 'At five thirty this morning.'

'So he went into the water an hour or two before midnight?'

Cowpar nodded affirmatively, his spectacles reflecting two orbs of light.

Hawksworth looked closely at the corpse. Though cleaned up for the examination, the body still had filth from the canal on it, strung in its hair, caught between its fingers. The body even smelled like the canal: the Klings often let their bullocks wallow and shit in its upper reaches. The fingertips of the corpse were already turning blue, as were its toes and the tip of its penis. Small fish had nibbled at the end of its nose, lips, eyelids. The scrotum had a large bite taken out of it. The eyeballs, shrivelled from the soaking, appeared collapsed, like crushed grapes. Hawksworth looked away.

'Have something to show you, Chief Detective Inspector.' Cowpar grasped the corpse's motionless head and twisted it towards himself. 'A blow to the side of the head, here, above the left ear.' He pointed to it.

It was as though the man's skull had caved in, resulting in a long concavity that had not broken the skin but had turned purple and scarlet.

'That looks nasty.'

'It would take quite a bit of force to cause that.'

'Do you think he was intentionally beaten?'

Cowpar shrugged. 'Possibly, although a stumble and fall could also cause that.'

They both stared down into the corpse's face. The dead man would never tell them what had caused this to happen.

'What about the nudity, Chief Detective Inspector? In all my years of service in the East, I have never had a white man delivered to me totally nude.'

'Perhaps he took off his clothes to go for a swim?'

Hawksworth looked at the polished fingernails, with muck from the canal stuffed underneath them, the clean white teeth visible through the contorted mouth, the fashionably cropped soft blond hair now fouled with globules and strings of indefinable organic matter. The man's clothes would have been expensive, Hawksworth decided, and a white band of skin on one of his fingers suggested that a ring had once been worn there habitually.

Had he gone into the canal nude, or had he been stripped of fine linen and pocket watch after he was discovered floating?

There was no way to be sure, unless his belongings were to somehow turn up now.

'Let us assume for a moment that this was not a case of stumble-and-fall. Is it possible to say with any certainty that the blow was struck before he went into the water?'

'You are suggesting that ...'

'That perhaps the blow had occurred after he was in the water.'

Cowpar leaned over the body, his nose and spectacles close to the wound. 'No, I cannot say.'

'So, it is possible that he was stumbling drunk, or fell in, or was pushed into the canal?'

'Or pushed along the waterfront on Beach Road, and then washed into the canal at high tide.'

'Then it is possible that he entered the water and managed somehow to strike the blow himself, by accident.'

'Yes, that is possible.'

'So we are looking at one of two possibilities: either he was struck on the head and pushed into the water then drowned, or he fell, or was pushed, into the water, then struck his own head.'

'Yes. The nudity?'

'Cannot be adequately explained. Someone did that to hide evidence perhaps. Or the body had been stripped prior to its discovery being reported.'

'We are looking at two possibilities then: his death was either a murder or an accident.'

'Or perhaps a combination of both: a brawl could have led to a fight, during which he was pushed, or slipped, into the canal, where he drowned. Then the body was stripped.'

'I cannot speculate, Chief Detective Inspector. All I can tell you about is the evidence I see before me. This man drowned. He has a nasty blow to the head that may or may not have occurred prior to his drowning, and that may or may not have been self-inflicted. The body was found nude. He is Caucasian, about our age, too, Chief Detective Inspector. As a coroner, that is all I can tell you.'

'But the death is to be treated as suspicious.'

Cowpar shrugged, as if to say 'you decide'. 'Is there a need for a further autopsy, Chief Detective Inspector?'

Hawksworth looked at the body again, at the drowned man who had met his fate in a distant land. He was a police matter now, one controlled by allocated manpower, budgets, reports, administrative procedure. 'There is no need for that, Dr. Cowpar. The man drowned in suspicious circumstances. That is enough to commence an investigation.'

'I will have to fill out a death report if we are to keep the body in custody – as evidence.'

'Yes.'

'At the present time, the cause of death cannot be ascertained.'

'No, it cannot.'

'But Chief Detective Inspector,' Cowpar said in slight exasperation, spectacles shining, 'I must enter a cause of death in the report if we are to keep the body in custody prior to burial.'

'Enter what you normally would enter under such circumstances. Follow procedure.'

The thick lenses flashed again as the coroner nodded his

assent.

'By the bye, what do you normally enter under such circumstances?'

The pearly light orbs of his spectacles turned towards the body on the slab and took in the blue fingertips, the twisted face, the smooth white skin already given to pooling fluid and putrefaction. 'The normal procedure? The cause of death is listed as "visitation of God".'

* * * *

The Chief Detective Inspector and Rizby were taking tiffin at a roadside stand that served *nasi lemak*, pan-fried egg, chicken meat, rice fried in the Malay style, served on a banana leaf with a spicy sauce called *sambal*. Hawksworth drank unsweetened hot black coffee; Rizby sipped on *teh tarik*, weak tea with condensed milk and sugar. Hawksworth finished describing the body of the drowned man to his adjutant.

'There were no marks on it save for the contusion caused by the skull, so we can rule out Chinese gangs.' The gangs tended to mutilate bodies before dumping them.

'What do you make of it, sir?'

'What do I make of it? You mean, what does my instinct tell me? The man was murdered. He was struck unconscious in a single blow then tossed into the water, probably not far from the mouth of the canal.'

'That is not far from the police station at Rochor.'

'For all we know it might have been one of our police that

killed him, Detective Inspector. In any event, he drifted through the waters in the dark of the night and when the body was spotted at dawn, it was stripped of its clothing and valuables and then reported found.'

'So we treat this case as a murder.'

'We must first establish who he is. Was. Then we will see if a murder investigation is in order.'

'He could have gotten drunk and fallen in.'

'The face on that man was not that of a drunkard. He looked like a slick fellow. His skin was, as they say, white as snow.' Hawksworth had never seen snow, so the expression he had heard from others since boyhood meant nothing to him. 'So he had either only recently moved here, to the equatorial zone, or he had somehow managed to stay out of the sun for long. Also, his nails and teeth and hair all seem well-kept; even his toenails are clipped and polished.'

'Where should we start looking, sir, to uncover his identity? Hotels and furnished rooms for merchant marine officers?'

'Yes, that would be good. Start with the luxury hotels, then work your way down.'

'The opposite of what we normally do, sir?'

'The corpse oozed affluence, even if of the grasping kind. The truly wealthy do not polish their toenails.'

'Any idea about his nationality, sir?'

The Chief Detective Inspector placed his empty cup next to the chicken bones and greasy paper, the only remains of his lunch. 'I would wager Australian or American, perhaps Canadian – not old Europe.'

'How could you tell?'

'The shape of the jaw. Our mixed-blood colonials and their American friends have developed square-shaped jaws, which rather look like shovels. Care to wager, Detective Inspector?'

Rizby finished his tea and the two men stood, the shorter one smiling. 'Alright, Chief Detective Inspector. I bet you one dollar that you are wrong. Not because I think you are, but only to keep the matter sporting.'

'Done,' they shook hands, with Hawksworth's seeming paw-like compared to Rizby's small dark one, which fit completely into his palm. 'Now take along some of the other detectives with you: Rajan Nair and, perhaps, Sher Iqbal, if you can find him. Then start searching the luxury hotels around High Street. And the Padang as well,' instructed Hawksworth, referring to the main green space that fronted the sea, a sort of parade-ground-cum-promenade that projected outward from the main town.

'Yes, sir. Will you be joining us?'

Hawksworth sighed, 'No, Detective Inspector, I will not. I have a report to start filling out.'

* * *

Several hours later, a knock came on Hawksworth's office door, and in stepped Rajan Nair. The man was half as old as Hawksworth was and only recently had been recruited to the position of Detective. He was now being unofficially tested for membership into Hawksworth's *burung helang*.

'Good afternoon, Detective.'

35

'Good afternoon, Chief Detective Inspector, sir. I have just returned from my patrol mission with Detective Inspector Rizby, sir.'

'Yes, I gathered as much. Do sit down and relax, Nair. There is no need to be nervous.'

'Yes, sir. I mean, no, sir, I mean ...'

'Just report, Detective.'

'Yes, sir,' and Nair remained standing, then spoke as if reciting from memory, 'Detective Inspector Rizby sent me to tell you that he believes that he has found the hotel room that the drowned man stayed in.'

'Very good.'

Silence.

'Is there any more, Detective?'

'Yes, sir. Detective Inspector Rizby has asked me to tell you that the man's belongings were found in Hotel Europa.'

'The Europa? Well, he must have been flashing cash.'

'Yes, Hotel Europa, sir,' Nair repeated, seemingly confused by the English colloquialism. His nose started to itch but he dared not scratch it lest the gesture be taken as a sign of disrespect and insubordination by his British superior.

'Anything else, Detective Nair?'

'Yes, sir, Detective Inspector Rizby asked me to tell you – to request you – to please join him at Hotel Europa.'

Hawksworth rose to his feet swiftly, causing Nair to take a step back. 'Come on then, Detective Nair, we are going for a ride together.'

'Sir?' Nair was practically trembling.

'To Hotel Europa,' and the taller man sailed past the detective and out of his office.

Nair followed, fiercely yet surreptitiously scratching his nose as he walked behind the Chief Detective Inspector, sighing with relief.

* * *

Hotel Europa was considered one of the most fashionable hotels in Singapore by newly arrived residents, with a clientele of visiting dignitaries, stage celebrities and wealthy businessmen on world tours. It was famous for its eggs-and-hash breakfasts and high-tea luncheons, and its Friday black-tie champagne lounge, where a Filipino string band played while the dance floor would become filled with the flitting dandies and social butterflies of the colony. However, despite the elegant decor, or perhaps because of it, the long-term European residents who tended to the conservative perspective viewed it as not so genteel, indeed meretricious, and stayed away from the place. Without being aware of it, Hawksworth was himself in this camp.

Rizby was waiting for him in the lobby, seated in one of the stuffed brocaded chairs, beside a potted palm. Several white customers walked past the small dark man, giving him looks of disdain. Sher Iqbal sat in the chair opposite the Detective Inspector, looking uncomfortable and disconcerted by the dazzling interior. The hotel manager, a petite man in a starched pink shirt, stood nearby, frowning. The Detective Inspector grinned when he saw Hawksworth walk in through the hotel's doors.

'Do not stand up, Detective Inspector Rizby. You look rather comfortable.'

'I am, Chief Detective Inspector, but, alas, I do not think that this hotel suits me.'

'Why would you say that?'

'Because the guests keep asking me to bring them their dinner,' he said loudly and then laughed, springing up from the seat.

Changing to a more serious tone, Hawksworth asked, 'So you think you have found our man?'

'Indeed, sir. We have been lucky, too, for this was the first hotel we checked. Room 203. Come and see?'

The hotel manager finally stepped into the conversation, 'You, sir, are the Chief Detective Inspector? I am Mr. Core, Manager of Hotel Europa.' He did not offer his hand.

'Yes?'

'Your ... assistant?'

'You mean, Detective Inspector Rizby?'

'Yes, your man informed me of the nature of your visit here. If indeed the situation proves to be as he has told me it is, I would appreciate it if your men would maintain a quieter presence. We would not want to disturb our guests unnecessarily.'

Hawksworth knew well what the manager meant, and that his concerns were not about the possible investigation of a murder at the hotel but about Rizby sitting in the lobby with his dark skin on display.

'My men are investigating a possible murder, Monsieur Core. And if indeed the murdered man was staying in your hotel, then your entire hotel staff will have to be interviewed. They might even be considered as possible suspects. And this includes you, Monsieur,' Hawksworth stepped towards the petite man. 'Have you ever been treated like a suspect in an investigation before?'

The man blanched. 'No, sir.'

'When the time comes, you will confess,' Hawksworth said with steely conviction, glaring at the manager.

'But, I have done nothing to confess,' he started to stammer, his hand reaching up to his collar, trying to loosen it.

Hawksworth, stinking of police work, dirt and food grease, stale sweat, and of his late morning visit to the dead house, leaned close enough to the manager to smell the man's treacly eau de cologne. 'Then you had better cooperate with my men and allow them the latitude necessary to perform their duties. Is your role in this investigation perfectly clear to you now?'

'Yes, sir. Yes, it is.'

'Then please lead us to Room 203.'

The party wound their way up a polished staircase to the second floor. The manager hurriedly unlocked the door to the room.

'You can go now, Mr. Core,' Hawksworth said as he and Rizby stepped into the room. 'Detective Iqbal, mind the door. Detective Nair, come inside with us.'

Room 203 was not luxurious by the standards of Hotel Europa; by the standards of most beds-for-rent in Singapore, however, it was Shangri la. The room had a private water-closet and a wash basin with a mirror on the wall above it; a large feather bed covered with lavender-coloured sheets; a polished rosewood bureau along with a matching chiffonier and wardrobe. The window looked down onto High Street – not the best of views but a breezy one nonetheless.

'Show me what you have found, Detective Inspector.'

Rizby opened the bureau and took out a pile of neatly stacked clothing, then placed it on the bed. The man's clothes were pricey stuff: two fine linen suits, seersucker day shirts and summer cotton trousers. They were also clean. 'He had his clothes laundered and pressed, but they were never worn after they were put in the drawers. And he had all of his clothes laundered.'

Hawksworth ran his hands over a linen jacket and observed that it was nicely tailored and did not feel like it had been worn much. He noted that the size of the jacket seemed a perfect fit for the body he had seen on the slab that morning.

'What else?'

'The labels on the clothes, they are all from the same tailor.'

Hawksworth opened the jacket. The label, sewn in red stitch into the lining, read 'Man's Wear. Charleston, South Carolina'.

'American?' Rizby asked.

Nair hesitated, then spoke, 'There is no passport.'

'Americans are not issued passports,' Hawksworth said plainly.

'But he was American, sir,' Rizby insisted.

'How do you know?'

'The hotel staff recognised the accent,' Nair said.

'And we did find these tucked into his luggage.' Rizby offered Hawksworth a stack of printed calling cards: 'J. Caramel. Neptune Ice Company, with offices in Boston and Savannah, USA.'

'And the luggage? How many pieces?'

'One, and it seems very much used. Also, there was this,' Rizby handed over two colour-picture postcards: one showed the Taj Mahal, while the other showed the Tank Road Train Station in Singapore. The backs of both the postcards did not have any writing on them.

'Nothing else? Wallet? Diary?'

'Nothing, sir.'

'So,' Hawksworth mused aloud, 'our man had been travelling in the tropics, perhaps across India. He travelled light to Singapore, perhaps expecting to only stay here for a short time. He could afford to stay in Hotel Europa but not in the best of its rooms. He possibly worked for an American ice company, and his clothes had been made in America.'

They locked the room behind them and returned to the lobby. Hawksworth leaned against a pillar. 'You interviewed the desk staff?'

'The man checked in yesterday morning. He had no reservation and only required the room for three nights. He left his clothes to be laundered, took breakfast in the lounge and left for the afternoon. Touring, he had said.'

'He must have gone to the Tank Road Station..'

'He returned to a late luncheon, then drank beer and played billiards until late in the evening. Then he went out again.'

'Presumably wearing the same suit as in the morning?'

'He only deposited his undergarments for cleaning in the afternoon. His other clothes had not been laundered yet.'

'And then?'

'And then he never came back.'

'What ship did he register as arriving on when he checked in?'

'Now it gets interesting, sir. The ship he had claimed to have arrived on did not dock here until today.'

Hawksworth moved across the lobby towards the billiard room. 'Find out if the attendant on duty today is the same man who served our deceased.'

It was the same man. The attendant also confirmed that the deceased spoke with an American accent. 'I knew because I had worked in America for several years.'

'Do you remember anything else about him?'

'No. He played billiards, not very well. He drank several mugs of beer.'

'Was he intoxicated when he left?'

'No, sir. Not even tipsy. He only drank two or three mugs.' The attendant paused for a moment. 'Also, he was new to the tropics, sir.'

'How do you know that?'

'Well, sir, you see, he sipped his beer, did not quaff it down as we have learned to do here to alleviate the heat.'

'Did he tell you about what had brought him to Singapore?'

'No, sir. He did not talk much at all. Certainly not much for an American. He did mention that he was in the ice trade.'

'Anything else?'

'Actually, there is one thing. He forgot to settle his bar bill yesterday, and we generally do not like our short-term guests to put things on their tab. Do you know where he is?'

'Yes, I do, and I do not think he is presently in any position to pay his bill.'

* * *

They sent Rajan Nair and Sher Iqbal home for the night, and Hawksworth spent half of the dollar Rizby lost to him on the wager to buy a beer for the Detective Inspector. Hawksworth ordered a stengah of whisky, a scotch and soda, with no ice, and watched his fox-like adjutant play a shot on the billiards table.

The balls cracked when Rizby took the lag shot. He placed his cue behind the baulk line, running his fingers over the green baize. The windows of the club opened into a dark courtyard, allowing a cool evening breeze to blow through. The men were alone, the room quiet except for the high-pitched staccato buzz of cicadas in the courtyard; from the street beyond came hawker calls and hoof beats, carriage-wheel squeaks and bullock snorts.

Hawksworth watched Rizby play as he spoke to him, 'Did our man die on his first night here in Singapore?'

'My belief is yes, he did. He lied about the ship he had taken to get here.'

'Or he simply forgot its name or got it wrong. Our clue is the calling card. It said "Neptune Ice Company". Perhaps he had planned to get here first, ahead of a shipment.'

'American ice does not come through Singapore much anymore.' Rizby cued a ball, his small frame cocked for the shot, his fox ears perking up. The shot struck the white ball into the red ball. 'Cannon,' he said with pride, under his breath.

'Well done, Detective Inspector.'

'So what is the next step, sir?'

'Pot the red.'

Rizby grinned and then did exactly that. He straightened himself, took a slug of beer that drained half his mug, and then offered the cue to Hawksworth. The tall man shook his head. The smaller man shrugged and re-set the table, then drained the rest of his beer.

'I suspect,' the Chief Detective Inspector said, 'that our deceased American was not here on legitimate business, but I need to prove this. Tomorrow I shall visit the Consulate and see if they know anything about him or Neptune Ice. In the meantime, you beat the bush and see if we can flush some more information about how our man arrived in Singapore. Find his ship.'

'Yes, sir. Sure you do not care for a quick game?'

'No, Detective Inspector, it is late and time for me to get home. Oh, and Rizby, care to wager another dollar? I bet that the American Consul knows nothing about the Neptune Ice Company.'

Rizby cocked his head and rubbed his earlobe. 'I cannot afford to lose another dollar. How about we wager for a mug of beer?'

'Done.'

As Hawksworth left, the night attendant went past him and towards Rizby, carrying another fresh mug of beer. He heard Rizby take another lag shot. Out on the street he headed through the broken shadows of the gaslight to the nearest hackney carriage station. The Chief Detective Inspector wished he had had another stengah to cushion the ride that lay ahead, to his home and lady in Geylang. The scotch might have also helped force the image of the drowned man's eyeballs, congealed like crushed grapes, from his mind.

CHAPTER III

Sailor Town to Battery Road

It was early morning, not long after sun up, as Hawksworth made his way through the silent streets of Sailor Town towards the heart of the commercial district.

The district was empty then, but by night the neighbourhood, consisting mostly of clapboard bars and tumble-down flophouses, was a riotous mess of pitifully drunken merchant-sailors, wandering prostitutes, con-artists and hustlers, gambling dens, arrack- and toddy shacks, and food sellers hawking their wares. Anyone who had the knack of plucking a few dollars from a sailor's chest could be found in the area. Royal Navy men were outright barred from the neighbourhood by shore patrols lest they soil Her Majesty's good name.

That morning, Hawksworth was taking the long way to the American Consulate – he needed a walk to clear his mind. The Chief Detective Inspector thought of the unblemished white skin of the dead American, his clean trimmed fingernails, his smooth face and stylish hair. He was not some sort of merchant sailor on shore leave; there was something about that face, it occurred to

Hawksworth in the silent squalor of Sailor Town, that seemed redolent of an upper class con-artist. Perhaps the man was a suspect and not a victim? But suspected of what crime?

Hawksworth walked beneath the colourful hand-painted tavern signs famous throughout Malaya. The Man on the Lookout featured a cheerful Jack Tar holding a gun backward, muzzle to his eye so that the weapon resembled a spyglass. Across the street was The Man at the Wheel, owned by the brother of the owner of The Lookout, whose sign was in direct intimation of the first, this one featuring a Jack Tar lashed spread-eagled on a ship's wheel, a drunken bewildered grin on his face. The two brothers, Italians, were forever at one another's throats about stealing prime wenches from each other's establishments – where the best girls went, the sailors were sure to follow.

Then there was The Hope and Anchor, owned by an Australian sea captain, where the main attraction were the Aussie bar girls, buxom lassies with hair golden like morning wheat or red-blazed like deep sunset, and with heaving cleavages that drove men to assault each other as they vied to get a grip on the ladies. One of the tavern's girls had grown so famous she had her gained her own slogan, echoed throughout the local seas: 'Jenny Hanse means romance.' The sensual Jenny in question, a lusty plump-thighed blonde with lavender eyes and a hearty laugh, eventually became such a threat to the peace and well-being of the men of the shipping and docking trades that she was none-too-politely packed away one night, put on a steamer bound home to Adelaide. By that point, two-dozen men had been maimed or killed in Jenny-related incidents.

Further on was the infamous Original Madras Bob. The tavern's sign had a white man embracing a dusky lady of indeterminate Oriental extraction dressed in Western ruffles and lace. It was a rough joint: a dance hall and saloon with an upstairs where the ladies could entertain clients with short-time love. The place had even been given a denunciatory description in a temperance movement pamphlet: 'It is an ordinary dance house, with a bar and glasses, and a dirty floor on which scores of women of all countries and shades of colour can be found dancing with Danes, Americans, Swedes, Spaniards, Russians, Negroes, Chinese, Malays, Italians and Portuguese in one hell-medley of abomination. The very sublimity of vice and degradation is here attainted, and the noisy scrapping of wheezing fiddles and the brawls of intoxicated sailors are the only sounds heard within its walls.'

Sailor Town ended abruptly at Cecil Street, where the land that had been reclaimed from the sea in 1879 had become stable enough for the road to be laid. Beyond this were mudflats, through which ran Robinson Road. There were no buildings on either side of the road, but only mud extending out towards the shore, boarded by the embankment. The mud stank with the organic stuff washed over the flatland at high tide and rotting quickly in the sun, the pervasive odour wafting over Sailor Town's night time revelries.

The reclamation flats had become a popular dumping ground for men killed in bar brawls. Police from the Telok Ayer Station would find these bodies in the morning, lying flat on their backs face up, with the sea lapping at the embankment a few feet away, as though they were sunbathing with their clothes on and their throats slit. Coolies were paid to collect the bodies, tossing them into the backs of covered carts for transport to the death house. If the American's body had been found here, it might have simply been discarded like a common sailor, Hawksworth mused. It was because he had been found in Rochor Canal that he had even come to Hawksworth's attention.

At the end of Robinson Road, at the entrance to the gentile commercial district, was the newly completed octagonal Telok Ayer Market, the burbling fountain at its centre and its ornate ironwork entrances at odds with its foul smells of fish and produce. Hawksworth stopped for coffee at a stall just inside the main entrance: *kopi-o kosong*, 'black, no sugar'. He sipped the hot brew, staring out at the reclamation flats.

He remembered what it had been like before, when the sea had washed all the way to Telok Ayer Street; sampans had beached on the shore before the gilt decoration of Thian Hock Keng temple, where the Chinese had offered smoky prayers to Ma Zu, the Hokkien goddess of the sea. Now the goddess was a quarter mile inland, and she would become further enclosed as the city extended its land further outward. The market where he now sipped the bitter coffee had been built on stilts over the water: many years ago, as a younger man, he had sat in nearly this same spot and dangled his legs over the rails, watching the tiny fish chase the crumbs that had been tossed from above. Reclamation was a funny word for what the city had done, Hawksworth mused. Was what was being reclaimed ever been taken in the first place? And once such a projection begins, where does it stop? To these questions, Hawksworth found no answers in the straight roadway that ran brightly through the stinking dark mud. He returned the empty porcelain cup to the Malay stall-keeper with a grateful '*terima kasih*' and headed into the commercial district, toward the American Consulate, and towards what he hoped would be definitive information about the corpse.

* * *

The transition was abrupt, as though the Telok Ayer Market were a giant turnstile from Sailor Town to the commercial centre, from the disreputable to the respectable. Here the wide streets bustled with all types of traffic, fleets of pedestrians and laden bullock-carts jostling with rickshaws, hackney carriages, horses and gigs.

The buildings around Raffles Place projected a stolidity that belied their box-like interiors. The facades were festooned with scaled ornamentation from different periods of European history: miniature Doric columns and man-sized Gothic cathedral windows were arranged side-by-side in neat rows, and Romanesque spires and baronial cupolas topped off the secular avenues. It was the polite architecture of a commercial empire.

A uniformed policeman saluted him as he passed the Kim Seng fountain, where men in suits paused to dip their hands in the cool water collected under the shade of young *angsana* trees, seeking relief from the late morning heat. Hawksworth wiped sweat from his eyes, immersed his solar topee in the fountain then dumped out the water before placing it again onto his head. By the time he had reached the door of the American Consulate, only a few hundred years away, his headgear was completely dry again, baked by the merciless sun.

The Consulate was being temporarily re-housed in a narrow commercial building while a grander structure was being erected for it on Beach Road. Despite the commercial frontage, the doors were opened by a porter in a peaked cap. The reception area was kept cool by the labour of a punkah puller, who sat on the floor, one leg raised in the air, where the cord tied to his foot ran up to the tasselled curtain swishing down from the ceiling. Two more men – all three appeared to be Bengali – sat in a row beside him, each tugging at ropes that swung the curtains over the heads of an audience assembled in the auditorium just off the main entrance. Hawksworth was peeking inside the open door of the auditorium when an eager Chinese clerk hurried up and enquired about his business at the Consulate; the Chief Detective Inspector explained, and the Chinese hurried silently away, pigtail swinging.

While he waited, Hawksworth leaned against the door jamb, listening to the flat, nasal voice of the speaker droning into the hot space, which was crowded mostly with ladies in flowery dresses, clearly the wives of officials, American or otherwise. It was the Consulate's turn to host the weekly luncheon lecture, a regular fixture in the social calendar of colonial ladies.

The little man in a starched collar behind the podium declaimed, red-faced in the stifling air, 'As the Tropics has been the cradle of humanity, the Temperate Zone has been the cradle and school of civilisation. Here nature has given much by withholding much. Here man found his birthright, the privilege of the struggle.'

The audience shifted in the squeaky wooden chairs, fanning themselves with the printed lecture notes as very un-ladylike sweat poured down their necks and backs.

'Today a certain peculiar type of climate prevails wherever civilisation is high. In the past the same type seems to have prevailed wherever a civilisation arose. Therefore, such a climate seems to be a necessary condition of great progress. It is not the cause of civilisation, for that lies infinitely deeper. Nor is it the only or even the most important condition. It is merely one of several. However, we may say that the civilisations of the Temperate Zone coincide with what we may also call the pinnacle of human progress. What we can be sure of is that the humanity of the Temperate Zone has produced the most refined civilisations, while those of the Tropics have progressed very little from the rudest state of humanity.'

The doors at the far end of the reception room opened, and the American Consul strode out. He spotted the Chief Detective Inspector and crossed over to him, his face set with a practiced expression that was meant to project conviviality and fellow-feeling. It was a look that the detective had seen on the faces of every highly placed official he had ever met. 'Chief Detective Inspector Hawksworth, welcome to the Consulate of the United States of America,' he shook his hand vigorously. 'Is this your first visit here?'

'No, sir, I once attended a reception given by your predecessor, a number of years ago.' The reception had been held by the previous man to ingratiate himself with the British authorities, something this new Consul, with his slick mane of blond hair and fashionably trimmed moustache had not had the presence of mind – nor the diplomatic inclination – to do.

'I see. I hope it's not trouble that brings you to our welcoming home today?'

'I am afraid so, sir, but we can wait until the lecture is over before we discuss the matter.'

'Did you have a chance to hear some of Dr. Dillinger's lecture? He's touring the Far East with the National Geographic Society.'

'I did hear some of it, sir. A very interesting perspective, indeed,' Hawksworth said politely but without a hint of sincerity.

'Yes, I myself would like to hear more of it, but unfortunately I'm a busy man today. What is it that I can assist you with?'

'The body of a white man was discovered yesterday and we believe the deceased was an American.'

The Consul's face remained impassive, his blue eyes emotionless. American seamen died in droves in Singapore.

Hawksworth continued, 'Because of the condition of the body, we suspect foul play. We also suspect that he was a businessman, perhaps even a well-connected one. He had registered at Hotel Europa.' The Chief Detective Inspector still did not get the reaction he sought. 'The body was found drowned in Rochor Canal. It was nude.'

'Nude?' The diplomatic face creased quickly and slightly, yet visibly in dismay. 'Oh, I see. Yes, that is terrible news. You say he was a businessman staying at Hotel Europa? Well, we'd better go on up to my office then.'

They wound up a narrow spiral staircase, past a second floor filled with secretaries seated at desks. Hawksworth caught a glimpse of a large-faced clock on the wall and of heads bowed down over ledgers. The heavy clack of typewriter keys faded as he followed the Consul up to the third floor, which seemed to consist only of his outer and inner office. A pretty brunette girl rose as they swung open the waist-high gate and walked through the reception area, into an unlocked door.

The office was Spartan by colonial standards. The Stars-and-Stripes flag hung limply from a stand in one corner; a sculpted bald-eagle motif in bas relief hung on the wall above a large oak desk that sat on lion's-paw legs. A plain sideboard held a decanter of brown liquor, most likely American whiskey. Two club chairs upholstered in green leather sat before the desk. Hawksworth waited for the invitation to sit in one: the invitation came as a hand gesture, a palm held upward and extended to the seat. The Consul took his seat in a swivel chair behind the desk. Hawksworth noted that the desk was devoid of any sort of paperwork or folders or any sign of active work. There was the usual pen and inkwell, a blotter pad, a small lamp, a heavy amber glass ashtray, sparkling and barren, and a bronze eagle statue in the same screaming pose as the bas relief that hung on the wall above it.

Matching this sleek emptiness was the Consul's creaseless face, which now gazed impassively at Hawksworth with a studied half-smile. Evidently, as the emissary of the colonial authorities, the policeman was expected to begin the conversation.

'I am sorry to trouble you with this business, but it would appear that the deceased in question was in Singapore working for an American company, the Neptune Ice Company.'

'And you say the body was discovered nude in Rochor Canal.

When was this?'

'The body was discovered yesterday at dawn. It is currently being held at the morgue at Sepoy Lines. We were only able to ascertain the deceased's identity late yesterday afternoon, when one of my detective squads searched and enquired at Hotel Europa.'

'That's exemplary work, Chief Detective Inspector! I would hope that our own police detectives would have done as well.' The blue eyes remained limpid and empty.

'Considering that he could afford to stay at Hotel Europa, we assumed that he might have stopped by the Consulate.' It was the habit of the well to do to pay a visit to their country's consulate upon first arriving in a new port.

'Not an unreasonable assumption, but I certainly don't remember meeting any visiting American businessman in the ice trade in the last few days. I'll have Cecilia check our registry and get back to you if we should spot anything out of the ordinary.'

'The name on the card was given simply as "J. Caramel". If it would be possible, perhaps, for the Consulate to check with your personnel in America, we would like to learn more about the man, and about the Neptune Ice Company as well.'

'I'm a little confused here, Chief Detective Inspector. Do you believe that this man was involved in criminal activity?'

'I should tell you that we are treating the matter as murder, not as an accidental drowning, sir.'

The Consul leaned back in his chair, his eyes narrowing on Hawksworth. 'This is very perturbing news. Of course, the Consulate will assist, in every way possible, with your investigation.'

'We only ask that you keep the story out of the American press while our investigation continues. And we would ask your assistance in contacting the man's employer and, hopefully, his family.'

'Of course! I'll have Cecilia send cables to ... Well, where did you say that this company located?'

Hawksworth took one of the business cards from the dead man's room and handed it across the desk. The Consul leaned forward to take it then reclined again in his chair, the springs squeaking. He read aloud: 'J. Caramel. Neptune. Boston and Savannah. Can't say that I'm familiar with this outfit, or with Boston or Savannah for that matter, but I'll have Cecilia cable home to learn more about this Mr. Caramel and the Neptune Ice Company. You can to hear from us about this in a day or two. And like I said, if there's any other way that we can assist you in your investigation, you just let me know.' His tone was collegial but communicated that the meeting was over. Hawksworth did not shift an inch, though: he wanted more playtime.

'The American ice trade here has somewhat diminished from what it once was.'

'Yes, unfortunately, the modern techniques for making ice with chemicals have superseded the ones we use for our home-grown variety – at least in this part of the world. I believe that the Singapore Ice Company was formed by ... Well, I am unable to recall the name of the outfit.'

'Boustead and Company.'

'Ah, yes. Boustead. Perhaps they know something about the

ice trade? Frankly, we don't much care about where the ice comes from so long as it keeps our drinks cold.' It was a friendly tone, but it delivered the same message: your time is up, Chief Detective Inspector.

'The old icehouse still stands by the river. It belonged to the Low family, Teochew Chinese, who used to deal with the American ice-trade. I imagine Boustead owns it now.'

The Consul said nothing, his practiced half smile still in place. This time Hawksworth took the cue. 'Thank you for your help today, sir. Hopefully we will be able to learn more about the identity of this ...' he paused, searching for an appropriate word, 'man.'

'I'm always happy to assist our British hosts in any manner I can. I suppose that if no one claims the body then it'll be laid to rest in a potter's field?'

'Potter's field, sir?' Hawksworth asked in a tone of bewilderment.

'Ah. Common grave?'

'Yes, the one meant for Europeans and ...' he recalled the nasal tone of the lecturer downstairs and added with a touch of sarcasm, 'other members of the Temperate Zone.'

Missing the inference, the Consul continued, 'How long will you keep the body in your custody before you bury it?'

'Not very long. One week, two at most. That too only if we know that there is family coming over to retrieve it. Bodies do not keep well in the tropics – even when we pack them in ice.'

The Consul was on surer footing when it came to commerce. 'Our ice trade may be diminished, but America has much else to offer our British cousins around the world, and America's very keen to increase its business, particularly in Singapore.' He pronounced the word as *singer-poor*. 'And you will keep me posted, Chief Detective Inspector, if any further information is discovered about this unfortunate affair? Pity the body will be buried in a common grave, but short of taking custody of it ourselves, I don't see what I can do about it.'

The man stood, the leather of his swivel chair showing the impress of his weight, his face still set in a diplomatic smile. The two men shook hands. He did not escort the Chief Detective Inspector out of his office.

'Keep me posted?' What the devil was that American expression supposed to mean, Hawksworth thought to himself with amusement.

* * *

In his office at the Central Police Station, Hawksworth recounted to Rizby his meeting with the Consul. 'Not a bit of concern about his own countryman. He did not ask about how the man died or if we had any suspects. He was concerned only about any possible costs that the Consulate might incur in taking custody of the body. Well, into the pauper's grave the nude American shall go.'

'You do not like Americans, sir?'

'Why do you say that?'

Rizby shrugged, his eyes mirthful. Hawksworth's tone had said it all.

'They like to view themselves as a historical inevitability. It was less than a century ago that we were at war with them. Now we are asked to embrace them as second cousins once removed. We are asked to politely accommodate their imperial ambitions at our own doorstep as they encroach in the Pacific, and we are asked to accommodate their criminality in our own home. You know well that Americans import much more than ice to Singapore.'

'Turkish opium.'

'And human cargo: coolies and prostitutes from the southern ports, whom they do not register with the Chinese Protectorate.'

They both fell silent, and then Rizby said, 'They do not import much ice any more. Why would an American ice merchant be here?'

The Chief Detective Inspector furrowed his brow. 'Telephone the Tanjong Pagar Dock Company and the Collector of Customs, and see if either was expecting an American ice ship – or for that matter, any American ships – in port over the last week. He might have come in via other means, but we shall start by eliminating the obvious.'

'Telephone, sir? Rather, could I simply send over a detective?'

Hawksworth sighed. Both men despised the telephone. Speaking into one was a painful process: it required shouting into a receiver, often repeating the same words a half a dozen times, while a disembodied voice answered from the other end, sounding like it was getting strangled inside a rusty trombone. Deciphering the uncanny dialogue was an acquired skill, and an unpleasant one at that. Nonetheless, it was faster than travelling to meet someone face-to-face.

'Yes, Detective Inspector, the telephone. We must embrace the changes that the engineers are thrusting upon us, or I am afraid that these same changes shall simply crush us and pass us by. The younger generation finds nothing opprobrious in a telephone conversation. In fact the younger officers clamour to use the device.'

'Then I shall get one to use it straight away, sir.'

'Good thinking, Rizby. After you do, we shall *makan*. Speaking with the American Consul gave me a powerful hunger that only home grown *nyonya laksa* will sate.'

'Home grown, sir?' Rizby asked, puzzled.

'An Americanism, Detective Inspector,' Hawksworth explained. 'An inevitable Americanism.'

* * *

After tiffin, the junior detective reported that the telephone had told them what they had expected to learn: neither the dock company nor the customs officials had expected an American ship to arrive in the past week, and none had.

With the official channels closed before him, the Chief Detective Inspector knew he would have to turn to his street sources. It was time, he thought with relish, to begin the job of detecting.

CHAPTER IV

The Mother-Flower Kongsi

DESPITE THE MYTH of the inscrutable East, Hawksworth had enough contacts throughout Singapore that few things remained secret to him for long. Often the secrets that did come his way were of little use, and often he knew it would be best not to interfere, but when it was time to direct a raid on an illegal brothel or opium den – those establishments that did not register with the Chinese Protectorate or were knowingly providing black market products – it was often Hawksworth's knowledge that helped the police swoop in.

He strode towards the heart of the Chinese quarter, a district he knew all too well: there was not a single alleyway or back staircase of the quarter that he was not familiar with. When Stamford Raffles had first set foot on the island in 1819, there had been a Chinese trading village located there; naturally, through the process of his compartmentalised, gridiron urban planning, the area came to be known as the 'Chinese quarter'. As immigrants from the mainland began to arrive there after the founding of the colony, the quarter was subdivided largely on the basis of the various dialect groups, each assigned to a street. The groups came from across the Chinese mainland, though mostly from coastal areas: Cantonese, Hokkien, Teochews, Hakka and many others. Divisions used to be sharp then, but as several generations of Singapore-born Chinese began mixing with the district's fresh arrivals, the dividing lines began to blur, the streets becoming more heterogeneous.

The other ethnicities of Singapore had mixed in as well. The South Indians had already established their places of worship – both Muslim and Hindu, side-by-side – on South Bridge Road, the quarter's main throughway. With its narrow square minarets and its Dravidian tower crowded with demonic figures, respectively, the Jamae Mosque and the Sri Mariamman Temple were popular destinations for visitors; groups of them could be found marvelling at the structures while dodging the steam trams running down the centre of the street. Picture postcards of the structures were sold at roadside shops – they confirmed a visual identity of the Orient that the European mind had conjured up long before, as did the nearby coolie market on Pagoda Street.

But now, at this hour of lavender dusk, as the softness of early evening was settling, the Chief Detective Inspector was the only white man visible on the street. There was no gaggle of visitors to impede his movement. They had gone back in to their hotels or were aboard their steamers, preparing for supper, not wandering the dusty native quarters. Once darkness had settled over the town completely, however, some of them – men, mostly – would be back for a few short hours to indulge in the more sensual attractions of the East that were offered in the nearby streets.

Hawksworth entered Almeida Street, which the local Hokkien called *gu chia chui hi hing au*, 'street behind the theatre,' for the Chinese opera house was located one street over. It was known to be a 'night street' because of its brothels, some of which featured Cantonese girls – who only serviced Chinese men – while others specialised in Japanese girls, known as *karayuki-san*, who serviced all-comers.

During the day the street bustled with rickshaw pullers and hawkers balancing their portable kitchens across their shoulders on bamboo poles, carrying cooking utensils and provisions. The shophouses, however, remained distinctly quiet and discreetly shuttered, laundry flapping in the sunlight above the dirt of the street, hanging from poles that jutted from second-storey windows. It was only after dark that the houses on the street would open to reveal signs of life.

Now, in twilight, as Hawksworth walked down the centre of the road, the traffic parted around him like water streaming around a rock. The road was usually muddy, but the prolonged drought had baked its red mud into a surface as hard as stone; the road had been left ridged in the middle where countless wheels had cut ruts into it when it had last been wet.

The long shadows of dusk began to draw out the night denizens from the warren of tiny subdivided rooms that lay behind the orderly façade of the shophouses. The shutters on an upstairs window opened and a pretty girl, her face without make-up, her hair in a bun, leaned out to shake the dust from a carpet. Smooth youthful male faces of the non-labouring classes began to peer from doorways and into the street, looking forward to the night.

Squatting against a pillar on the five-foot-way, the arcade that lined the street, about half way down the block, was a thick-set Chinese, his muscular arms folded across his chest, his queue coiled around his neck. He was dressed in a tight purple silk vest embroidered with a blue dragon over a loose black *changshan*. On his head was a straw boater hat with a black silk band that shaded his eyes as he stared intently at the faces of the passers-by. Despite the dirt of the street, his clothes were immaculate. They were also expensive. He was dressed for entertaining.

His eyes darted to the figure of the white man approaching him, and his purple lips slid into a smirk before he stood up. Hawksworth watched as the Chinese slipped into the shadow of the five-foot-way.

Hawksworth knew the man well. He was Tan Yong Seng, head of the muscle of the *Ah Boo-Hway kongsi*, one of the so-called secret societies that functioned like a combination of a criminal gang, a fraternal guild and a mutual aid society. The colonial authorities found that the *kapitans* of these societies were useful liaisons to the Chinese community, but their involvement in black market trading and human trafficking eventually made the devil's bargain too unsavoury for the British administrators' palates. The government, attempting to outright ban the societies, passed an ordinance in 1890 that gave police the power to arrest suspected members and raid houses on the flimsiest of pretexts.

Of course this edict only drove the societies further underground, beyond the control of the authorities. Old Malaya hands had warned that this would be the precise outcome of such legislation, but they had been ignored. Hawksworth risked official censure if his friendship with Yong Seng, and his association with the Mother-Flower *kongsi*, as the Hokkien was rendered in English, ever became known.

He had first encountered then befriended the stouter man nearly a dozen years earlier, when Yong Seng fell nearly dead drunk at his feet at the gate of the Chinese cemetery at the poorly lit junction of South Bridge Road and Tanjong Pagar Road. He had been far too drunk on rice wine, weaving through traffic with his arms swinging, to notice that he was on a collision course with a white man in a blue serge uniform, for Hawksworth was yet to be made detective.

When he slammed into Hawksworth, he nearly knocked him down.

The truncheon in the taller man's hand was cocked to give the drunkard a skull-cracking blow, but when Yong Seng rolled over and showed his face, Hawksworth froze. The face staring up at him was not of a drunken native who needed a thrashing but that of a young boy Hawksworth had known in Georgetown in his own youth, a young boy from the market place that he had been incredibly cruel to. Given his relatively higher standing in the social order, Hawksworth had never been punished for this cruelty, but his actions still haunted him. Yong Seng was not that same boy, and perhaps he did not even look much like him, but in that sudden moment of collision and potential retribution, Hawksworth found the chance to redeem himself. He helped the drunken stranger to his feet, and then walked him all the way to the *kongsi* house, at the time located on Hokkien Street.

After Hawksworth had deposited the man at the door,

another Chinese man had appeared, enormously fat, and thanked Hawksworth for delivering his cousin safely, then asked the constable his name. The following afternoon, Yong Seng presented himself at the Central Station – stinking of vinegary wine sweat – with an apology, some profuse thanks and a token handful of *kepengs*, Chinese coins. Hawksworth responded by buying the terribly hung-over man tiffin from a stall on Macao Street. Yong Seng responded to this additional kindness by taking Hawksworth back to the *kongsi* house on Hokkien Street, where seated in a private room, filled by the ethereal strains of a girl's soft voice and the snakeskin *erhu* she bowed, they proceeded to chatter and laugh and drink themselves into a stupor from which it took Hawksworth two full days to recover. They had been fast and loyal friends ever since.

Yong Seng's family had migrated to Singapore from their ancestral home, a fishing village on a small island in the Formosa Straits, but Yong Seng himself had been born and raised in a local kampong. Although lacking the most basic of education, he had learned the languages he had needed to know to survive on the rough Singapore streets: he spoke not only his native Hokkien but also Cantonese and Teochew as well as Malay, a little Tamil and even a smattering of Siamese. Also, crucially, he spoke English, and spoke it almost fluently. Although the same age as Hawksworth, he now looked much older; his once cherubic face, smooth and pudgy cheeked, was now ravaged and pitted from decades of consuming rice wine and being exposed to the deleterious miasma of the densely packed Chinese quarter.

The taller man stepped into the sudden shade of the five-foot-way, seeking that very face. Yong Seng leaned casually against the red Chinese letters painted onto the doorframe of the *kongsi* house. Hawksworth exchanged a glance with his old friend, who, in turn, nodded then pushed open the hinged half-length doors that barred entrance to the darkened front room. He stepped in, his *changshan* swishing like a priest's soutane. Hawksworth followed him quickly.

In the front room were altars that held statues of the graceful Ma Zu, the sea goddess, and the fierce scarlet-faced warrior Guan Yu, the deity worshipped by those whose traffic required honour and loyalty among brothers-in-arms. Hawksworth noted another shrine, placed on a lower altar, this one dedicated to Pan Chin Lien, the sweet-faced patron spirit of prostitutes.

In the dimness of the room, they greeted each other in the mishmash of Malay and English that was the lingua franca of the Straits: '*Selamat malam*, Yong Seng.'

'*Malam*, Chief Detective Inspector. How are you?'

'I am well, thank you for asking. How are you?' Hawksworth switched to English.

'*Boleh, boleh tahan*. Better for seeing you. You have not come here in a long time.'

'That is true. Do not take offence. My woman often keeps me at home.'

The Chinese face cracked into a mirthful smile. 'No more late nights with your friends?'

'We will do that soon again, old friend. But today, I am sad to say that I have come here on business.'

'Police business?'

'An investigation. A dead *ang-moh*. Washed up in Rochor Canal yesterday morning. We believe he is American. And I know that the Mother-Flowers do business with Americans from time to time.'

The mirthful look stayed in place, but even in the murky room Hawksworth could see the light shift in Yong Seng's eyes. Hawksworth was always welcome with Yong Seng as a friend, but not always as a detective.

The Mother-Flower *kongsi* was a relatively new clan, its membership mostly Hokkien, with the founding fathers and those holding upper ranks first-generation Singaporeans. They had moved their *kongsi* house into what had once been a street dominated by Cantonese societies to make two points. One, they were no longer part of the old guard of societies that had come from their home province of Fujian and had established branches in Singapore. They were, as the Americans would say, 'home grown'. Two, they wanted to show the other dialect groups, by setting up shop within an enemy camp, that they were serious competition.

In truth, most of the societies did business with each other on a regular basis, and so long as one another's turf was respected, everyone could prosper. But when times were lean, or when someone got greedy, the knives would have to come out. Factionalism was rife even within dialect groups. Police pressure simply fractured them further.

Yet, Yong Seng and the Chief Detective Inspector both found their relationship to be mutually beneficial. Hawksworth could ply the Mother-Flowers for information; they could, in turn, use

Hawksworth's connections and influence to further their own ends. Hawksworth was not above alerting them of impending police actions in exchange for useful gossip about the upper echelon of the Chinese societies.

'You want to know about our business with Americans?' Yong Seng asked.

'I already know about your business with Americans. I would like to know about any business you had with this particular American. The dead one. Not that I think you had anything to do with his death.'

'Ha!' Yong Seng laughed the harsh Chinese laugh that meant rueful mirth then continued in a tone of retrospection, 'I have never killed a white man. If you want to know about our business with Americans, come upstairs, my friend. Yong Chern is there.'

The house was oddly still: its residents, mostly prostitutes from southern and eastern China, were just starting to wake up in their curtained rooms. From the front parlour, the two men ascended a narrow staircase that opened onto even narrower hallways on the second and third floors. There were rows of doors on the second floor and only curtained partitions on the third. The first floor was for gambling and opium smoking. The second floor was where the girls slept and where, after dark, the greasy nudity occurred. The house was illegal, as it was not registered as a licensed brothel with the authorities. Rather, visitors gained access to it only through association with the Mother-Flowers; in effect, the upscale house largely served as a clubhouse for the members of the *kongsi*.

Hawksworth followed Yong Seng to the uppermost room, an

attic space that functioned as a private office, far enough from the pit latrine on the ground floor that the nauseating stench did not reach it. Chong Yong Chern was the master of the house and the *samseng thau*, or middle boss, and he ran the Mother-Flower's gambling and prostitution rackets. Hawksworth lacked such easy access to the *samseng ong*, the chief of the Mother-Flower *kongsi*, whom he had never met. They opened the thin bamboo door and entered a small space, a room with a gabled roof and exposed rafters overhead. A desk with an abacus, some pens and papers, and an oil lamp stood in one corner of the office. The walls were bare except for one white scroll with Chinese characters hand-painted onto it in black ink; Hawksworth could not decipher what the characters meant. For his lifetime in the Malaya, he had learned only scattered phrases in Chinese – mostly curse words and common expressions – while the written ciphers of Chinese words eluded him completely.

Seated on a low divan of carved rosewood inlaid with mother-of-pearl was a massively fat man wrapped in a plain blue *changshan* that spilled luxuriously around his corpulent frame. His queue was undone, spilling in a black cascade around his shoulders. He was fanning his face impassively when they entered: the face abruptly creased into a wide smile when he saw the tall white man.

'Chief Detective Inspector Hawksworth!' Yong Chern bellowed in heavily accented English. 'What a great surprise! I am so pleased to see you!'

The room was oppressively hot, thick with smoke from the joss sticks that had been lit to perfume the air, and from the cheroot burning in the mouth of the middle boss, and from the ornamented glass water-pipe, what the Arabs called 'shisha' and the Indians 'hookah,' in the mouth of a petite girl sprawled by his feet on the polished wood floor. The only light came through the slats of a wooden shutter, and Hawksworth had to peer intensely in the dimness to discern a low chair and table beside the divan.

'Hello, Yong Chern. It is good to see you again,' Hawksworth said as he casually assumed the chair.

The big Chinese smiled broadly, the cheroot hanging from his mouth, and rang a small bell on the divan, reaching past his bulky frame. Yong Seng remained standing near the door frame, his straw boater still resting snugly on his head.

Switching to Malay, a language in which he could converse far more fluently, Yong Chern said, 'What brings you to us today, Chief Detective Inspector? Are you in the mood for some of the pleasures of the house?' he laughed loud enough to shake the rafters.

As if on cue, the girl took a long puff off the tube that snaked up from the water pipe and then exhaled into the centre of the room: the blue smoke hung heavily in the slated beams of late afternoon sunlight. While Hawksworth stared intently at her, an older woman entered the room – it was the mother of the house. Yong Chern spoke quickly in Hokkien to the woman: Hawksworth knew that tea or other condiments would be served shortly to him. Only then would the men begin to speak in earnest.

'I see you are looking at the girl.'

'She is smoking bhang?'

'Yes. Would you care for some?'

Hawksworth politely refused. He had smoked bhang once before and had found its effects pleasing: the mild hallucinogenic, made from female cannabis flowers and imported from India, produced an effect akin to drinking strong wine, but without causing any trauma to the stomach. Tonight he needed his head clear, and given the heat and dimness of the room, he would already have enough difficulty staying focused.

The girl shifted on her cushions, then tucked her legs beneath her firm backside. She was wearing only a loose white shift of cotton over baggy trousers made of the same material, yet, by the way she sinuously curled her body, Hawksworth was able to make out the supple curves of her petite frame.

Noticing his interest, Yong Chern spoke gently in Hokkien, 'Zhou Shu En, sit up and greet our esteemed guest.'

Stretching like a lazy feline, Shu En, still dazed, looked up, and it was only then did she notice the white man: her eyes widened in surprise, and then she greeted Hawksworth in Hokkien, with the Chief Inspector Detective responding in English.

Hawksworth would later learn from Yong Seng that she had been sold by her parents as a *mui tsai,* or 'little sister'. Usually, their role would be as unpaid domestic servants, but a female child as uniquely pretty as Shu En would most assuredly have fetched a high price and be destined for a life in prostitution. When Yong Chern saw her, he had decided he would keep her for himself.

The elderly house mother returned and set a tray on the table. Despite the tropical heat, on it was a small pot of hot tea and a room-temperature bottle of rice wine. Hawksworth pointed to the tea, and the mother poured a cup for him, and one each for

Yong Seng and Yong Chern. The three men ritually clacked their cups and then took a swig. Business would commence soon.

Hawksworth was aware that the girl was eyeing him with the wary curiosity a kitten displays when she encounters a puppy for the first time. She could not have been more than sixteen or seventeen; this was old for a *mui tsai* girl, and Hawksworth wondered how long she had been passed on from one owner to another before Yong Chern had received her.

Stroking the hair on her small skull, Yong Chern said, 'She has never been this close to a white man before. Forgive her for staring.'

The bhang had glazed her rook-black eyes and frozen her face in a gaze of enchantment, making her look as though she had just tumbled out of a fairy painting. A lock of jet-black hair fell away from the bun piled atop her head onto her cheek, painting a dark curlicue against her pearl-white skin. Unusual for a Chinese woman, her lips were coral pink, Hawksworth noticed. Turning to face Yong Seng, he said in Malay, 'She is very pretty. Take care of her.'

Yong Seng snorted the Chinese snort that meant humour at the obvious. 'Shu En,' he addressed the girl in Hokkien, 'he says that you are pretty.'

The pixie eyes scrutinised the white man more closely. Noticing the hair on the back of his hands, she asked, 'Is he furry all over? Like a monkey?'

Yong Chern burst out loudly in the Chinese laugh that denoted outright humour. 'She said—'

Hawksworth cut him off. 'I heard her,' he said in English. His

Hokkien was limited, but he was still able to follow her meaning. 'Tell her that I have hair where normal men have hair, and no place else.'

Yong Chern did so. The girl's gaze of enchantment did not dissipate as she further appraised Hawksworth. 'Yet he smells like a water buffalo.'

Both Yong Chern and Yong Seng nearly doubled over in laughter. Hawksworth did not understand the comment in a literal way, but again, he guessed at its meaning. However, the girl's glassy gaze and fine doll-like beauty made it difficult to summon his anger. Despite himself, he found himself hoping to see the girl again. The wishful desire that quickly followed this thought, as he stole one more glance at the coral pink lips, was repressed with much effort.

As the laughter of the men subsided, the girl turned back to her bhang pipe. Yong Chern spoke first, 'So, Chief Detective Inspector, if you did not come here to make merry, what business can we do for you today?'

Yong Seng spoke rapidly in Hokkien, 'He wants to know about the dead American.'

Yong Chern stroked his chin then stared at the wooden ceiling. 'Americans,' he said loudly in English, 'only bring three things to Singapore: ice, opium and poor Chinese looking for work.'

'Yes, I know. And I know that the Mother-Flowers often work closely with them in the black markets for opium and coolie labour.'

'Ah! Yes, opium. American opium. American opium that the American sailors bring from Istanbul.'

'We both know that the Mother-Flowers have a large share of the underground American opium trade.'

'So you come to see me when Americans come to Singapore?' Yong Chern smiled slyly, pronouncing the last word as *si-ga-po*.

'When Americans come to Singapore and are pulled dead from Rochor Canal, I turn to my brothers and friends, who know Americans. Supposedly, this American was working in the ice trade. Did he also, perhaps, work in the opium trade?'

Yong Chern and Yong Seng exchanged knowing glances before the latter suddenly shouted, 'British opium is shit! You let the Hai San clan control the opium farm. They bring in opium for the black market, too! Because they can make more money if they double their imports. The opium farm does not earn them half of what they make in black market opium. Yet the British do nothing. I say, let the Americans come! Better the Americans than the Hai San!'

The Hai San were a Cantonese clan, the most powerful *kongsi* between Singapore and Penang, and the biggest players in the Chinese vice trade. They were known to be especially vicious and maintained their place at the top by either co-opting or intimidating – or killing off – the other clans in the Straits colonies.

Hawksworth sighed at the outburst. He had to endure such tantrums nearly every time he met his Hokkien friends. 'I have no control over the opium farm – you know that. As for the Hai San, I have no influence with them. You, the Mother-Flower clan, you are my ... concern.' He chose this final word carefully.

'The Hai San buy big dogs – policemen – like they are steamed buns!' Yong Chern spoke quietly but snubbed out his cheroot vehemently.

The moment had turned tense. The girl sat quietly, staring at her water pipe. Hawksworth spoke first, 'I cannot provide answers about police corruption or your on-going attempts to claim a portion of the Hai San's trade. However, if they are also dealing with Americans, then, perhaps, I could begin making inquiries with them as well.'

Now it was Yong Chern's turn to sigh. Yong Seng stepped forward with another cheroot for his boss. Yong Chern puffed several times as if deep in thought, then spoke, 'We know about the dead American. But he was not working for us. He was not working for the Hai San either. No one knows why he was here or why he died. Perhaps it was merely fate?'

'What do you know about him?'

'We know how he got to Singapore. Nothing more.'

'How did he come here?'

'By ship, from Batavia. The ship docked yesterday morning at Beach Road for repairs. It was here to deliver Turkish opium to the Low family *kongsi*. One of our brothers watched a white man get off the ship; the man had with him only one bag.'

'Why was your brother watching the ships at Beach Road?'

Yong Chern gave Hawksworth a withering look, as if to say, 'All the clans watch each other all the time, and we have no choice but to do this —you are well-aware of this'.

'The Low and the Hai San are forming an alliance. One will control the opium farm, the other the spirit farm. They will co-operate in the black-market trade of both.'

'A joint monopoly?'

'Yes. We cannot allow this to happen. So we watch their traffic very closely.'

'One more question: do you know if the ship is still berthed at Beach Road?'

Yong Chern nodded affirmatively, then pandiculated his large, soft body further into the hard sofa, the cheroot dangling from his mouth, his loose hair snaking across his remarkable belly. 'It is still there, due to depart tonight. If you hurry, you can still catch it. Please do not alert the Marine Police to the illegal landing and off-loading. The ship captain is a friend of ours – a Javanese. That is how we knew the opium was coming for the Lows.'

Hawksworth nodded his agreement then turned to leave, with Yong Seng walking right behind him, but before he could descend the stairs, Yong Chern called out to him. With one fat brown hand gently stroking Shu En's silken hair, the middle boss said, 'The Lows are Teochew; the Hai San are Cantonese; but the Mother-Flowers are Hokkien. Not today, not even perhaps next year, but soon, and then forever, Singapore will belong to us.'

Hawksworth opened his mouth to retort something about Her Majesty's Royal Navy, but Yong Chern cut him short: 'Hurry, Chief Detective Inspector, or you will miss your ship.'

The last thing Hawksworth saw in the smoky room before he dashed down the narrow flight of stairs was the girl's pixie-faced gaze, her luminous skin glowing like the moon in the room's dimness as her dark eyes met his own.

* * * *

Hawksworth exploded out of the front door, nearly colliding with a gaggle of shirtless Tamil workmen. He spotted a rickshaw puller at the front of the house, snoozing in his conveyance, his feet propped onto the crossbar, his hat resting low on his head.

'Rickshaw! Boy!' he yelled, and in a twinkling the statue-still figure jerked to life and grasped the pulling bar to come into his starting position. Hawksworth swung himself into the seat and, without bothering to pull the canopy over his head, shouted, 'Beach Road!' They were off in a shot, the nimble body of the puller dodging the sharp ruts in the hard red mud of the street.

The rickshaw wallah went over Elgin Bridge and plunged into the evening traffic clustered on North Bridge Road, but he was forced to slow down, picking his way through the perpetually changing density, thick with hackney carriages and other rickshaws.

It was little more than a mile and a half to the quay at Beach Road. 'Faster, damn you, run faster!' Hawksworth yelled, shielding his face from the dust. They were slowed again by the ponderous black behemoth of a soot-belching steam tram. 'Run around it!' Several passengers pointed at Hawksworth from the open deck as he bellowed at the rickshaw wallah, leaning forward. Rounding the tram, they nearly rammed directly into a load of carrots, a wall of orange spikes, stacked high on the back of a pony cart. Slipping past this obstacle, the puller began to run even faster, the road suddenly open before him as pedestrians leapt out of the way. The only sounds in Hawksworth's ears were the man's panting and the spinning of the wheels within their greased hubs and the dull grinding of the rims as they crunched at high speed through the compacted dirt of the road. The puller did not slow down for another two blocks, until they had entered the Malay quarter.

They rounded Sambawa Road and were given a straight view all the way down to Beach Road: the masts of ships under repair could be seen against the pink sky of the tropical twilight. As they drew closer, Hawksworth realised there was a commotion along the quayside. Coolies were running frantically, heaving sacks on their shoulders and bumping into bullock carts, causing the bulls to bellow out in panic.

He could smell the acrid smoke before he could see it. The rickshaw came to a halt, and as Hawksworth leapt out, he could see the ship burning one block away at the mouth of the river. The coolies were frantically emptying the storehouses lest the fire spread and destroy the stock; the shop owners were wild eyed, yelling orders as the coolies dashed in and out of the godowns and store fronts.

Hawksworth began pushing through the melee. He towered over the frantic mob, ordering them to clear the way as he ran towards the burning craft.

The smoke was growing thicker as he shoved his way closer: the craft had only recently burst into a full conflagration. As he neared it, eyes watering, he watched two shirtless coolies quickly hacking away at the rope that held the ship to the shore. Finally, the rope was cut, and a crowd of coolies rushed forward with oars and poles in a coordinated effort to shove the craft further into the water, away from the quayside and the adjacent crafts. Braving the heat and noxious smoke, shouting all the while as they heaved, the crew pushed the fireship into open water.

As the ship turned away from the shore, one of her masts cracked, and then snapped as the rigging burnt away, and smoke poured from her hold. Cinders and feathery ashes began to fall onto the crowd. As he shook the soot off his sleeve, while holding a handkerchief over his nose and mouth, Hawksworth felt something hot brush past his ear: a flaming ball with wings smashed into his shoulder. The man next to him started flailing at something hot stuck to his shirt, his long queue flying about him. In an instant, the whole air seemed to be filled with hot sticky bombs that thumped into the horrified mob, which began to stomp its feet and flail its arms in a vain effort to keep the horrible invaders away, cursing and screaming and offering short prayers against this heinous new form of devilry.

Cockroaches were raining down from the ship, Hawksworth realised. Ignited by the fire, the insects were flying into the crowd. The assault lasted only a few minutes, but it was enough to thin the mob of coolies, who retreated into the godowns and shophouses along the quayside, madly slapping at the white blobs of stinking bug fat clinging to their clothes and hair.

Meanwhile, the ship drifted out into the river current, which pushed it away from the quay and towards the kampong made of wood and the *attap* huts that stood on brick stilts on the mud flat on the opposite shore near the Kallang River. If it reached those houses, the whole village would surely burn down. Such disaster was averted though as two, at first, then four, then a dozen small skiff-like *kolehs* and sampans glided as close as they dared to the burning ship, which was now reduced to a smoking hull, its masts fallen away, its upper deck collapsed.

Shirtless occupants held long bamboo poles at the prow of the *kolehs* while their companions paddled with all their might from the back of the boats. With shouted coordination, they finally managed to push the flaming hulk into the open water of the Kallang Basin: it burnt to the waterline then sunk, the thick keel upended, like a burnt out matchstick, and stuck into the bottom mud.

The fire brigade appeared and turned its attention to stamping down the smaller fires that the falling embers had sparked among the other wooden crafts tied along the quayside. Farther along Beach Road, a crowd gathered from the nearby market to watch the remains of the ship burn into the basin. The orange of the flames reflected in the water was becoming more lurid as the sky changed into the violet darkness of late evening. Less than thirty minutes had elapsed between Hawksworth's arrival at the quayside and the ship burning itself out.

The Chief Detective Inspector could identify the type of craft: it was a twin-masted *phinisi*, a Bugis ship typically used to transport light cargo throughout the region. Sturdy and swift, *phinisi* were favoured by captains complicit in the black market trade all over the South China Sea.

A Malay constable from the Rochor Police Station, located nearby on Crawford Street, had appeared by Hawksworth's side. Without taking his eyes off the flaming hulk, the Chief Detective Inspector asked, 'When did that ship arrive?'

'About two or three days ago, sir.'

'Was any one aboard the ship when it caught fire? Any sign

of the captain or crew?'

'I do not know, sir.'

'Well, then,' Hawksworth turned to look down into the face of the constable, who, in turn, seemed completely transfixed by the spectacle before them, 'do you not think it would be a good idea to find out?'

The constable looked up at the white man, frozen for a moment in incomprehension, and then said, 'Yes, sir, of course,' but he did not move.

Hawksworth sighed and made his way to the nearby station. Later he would have to give a statement. As for now, the station duty officer would need to take control of the crowd and begin to restore some semblance of order.

As the tall man wearily strode up Crawford Street, a wiry figure suddenly stepped into his path. Hawksworth tried to walk around the man, who he now saw was a Chinese with a narrow chest and spindly legs. The man, however, began to yell something at Hawksworth, and the Chief Detective Inspector reached under his jacket for his truncheon. The figure was now jumping up and down in the lowering darkness and demanding something from Hawksworth in a shrill Chinese dialect he did not know. Pushing the strange man until his back was forced against a warehouse wall, Hawksworth peered more closely at him, and only then did he recognise the rickshaw puller who had carried him to the quayside from Almeida Street. What the man wanted was to be paid. In his rush, Hawksworth had dashed off without paying his bill. Despite the spectacular scene of calamity at the quayside, the puller was not about to let his fare simply melt into the crowd.

Bemused, Hawksworth paid the man, who dashed away into the gloom, disappearing as quickly as he had appeared. Normally, the Chief Detective Inspector would have burst out laughing at the temerity of the puller, but tonight his mind was already elsewhere, casting back over the day that had passed while already planning his next move for the morning.

Amidst all that commotion and noise, while he had been closest to the fire, fully engulfed in smoke and cinders, with insects exploding around him, Hawksworth had noticed something he decided he would not mention in his official statement about the incident. He had been unable to detect the faintest odour of opium coming from the burning ship: either the illicit cargo had all been removed or that ship was not carrying any of the vile stuff. And ice does not burn, he noted grimly.

CHAPTER V

Panglima Prang

THE NEXT MORNING'S EDITION of *The Straits Mail* was quick to capitalise on the tragedy:

Yesterday evening, the most spectacular conflagration to occur in Singapore since the burning of the coal sheds at Tanjong Pagar took place at the boat repair yards near Beach Road. A native craft caught fire and burnt to its hull before tipping upright and slipping beneath the waves. The charred hulk of this craft can still be seen protruding from the water near the Marine Police Station on Tanjong Rhu.

The fire began aboard the ship that had arrived from Batavia only two days ago and had stopped at the Rochor wharf for repairs at the boat building yard of Ho Ah Cheong. The boat burnt for nearly thirty minutes and attracted a great crowd of spectators up and down the seafront. From Johnson's Pier, an enormous volume of black smoke could be seen rising from Kallang Basin. Superintendent Owen and the fire brigade came early on the scene, but naturally could do little to stay the burning.

A greater catastrophe was narrowly avoided. The Malay

kampong and wooden shipyards on Tanjong Rhu appeared in danger of grave mishap after the burning ship was cast adrift from its moorings. Due to the presence of mind and bravery of the native population, the vessel was pushed away from the kampong and into the harbour in the nick of time.

The only loss of life would appear to be the ship's captain, whose badly charred body was found early this morning washed up near the Padang. The police are said to be investigating the origin of the fire, which is believed to have been started by the captain himself.

The young reporter had stopped by the station at Rochor while Hawksworth was still on the scene. Taking notes by gaslight, the reporter listened to the Chief Detective Inspector's statement and intently scribbled down all that the police had thus far been able to piece together. The Chief Detective Inspector told the newspaper man the truth and the entire story, as much of it as he understood, but he intentionally left out the missing pieces. And the reporter, unschooled in the latest trends of muckraking journalism, declined to press for more information than what he was given. He reported what he had been told, nothing more.

There was no mention of the Chief Detective Inspector's suspicions that the ship was involved in carrying out opium smuggling for the Lows, or that a white man had sneaked into Singapore aboard the same ship – and had been murdered only a few hours later. The very mysterious fact that, except for the dead captain, the crew of the vessel remained unaccounted for – and were still missing – would also be withheld.

Often these Bugis vessels, carrying a cargo of legitimate

goods, would stop in the straits, beyond sight of the port, then tie up with a vessel carrying American opium and mix in some of the illicit stuff with their own licit goods.

But the presence of the white man was more difficult to explain, assuming that he was indeed attached to the ship; however, the man getting washed up in Rochor Canal only two days before the ship had burnt down was too much of a coincidence. Whoever had disposed of the American had also disposed of the ship, Hawksworth was convinced, and all of that was a great deal of trouble and expense to go through in order to erase the evidence of smuggling a dozen or so crates of opium balls.

If Yong Chern was right and the ship had been bringing in illegal opium for the Low clan, then surely the Lows could somehow be implicated in the death of the American and, perhaps, the intentional burning of the ship? Murder and arson were no petty crimes, but then again the Low family were no petty criminals. The family members were not very likely to get their own hands dirty though; they could employ any number of hooligans to do their bidding, of course.

Nonetheless, after weighing the matter over his morning cup of *kopi-o kosong*, he decided he would pay a visit to the Low family. They owed him a favour, and this might be the time to call it in.

Stalking out of his office into the blazing saffron sky of a cloudless late morning, Hawksworth hailed a passing rickshaw and climbed abroad it. It would be best for him to pay his visit alone. The Lows were a powerful family in Malaya and to even suggest to their face that they were somehow involved in this nefarious business, despite the fact of their involvement being an open secret, would require deft skill and a mind that could move swiftly from East to West and back again.

* * *

Chinese from the coastal provinces of the mainland had maintained a presence in the Straits for centuries prior to the arrival of the Europeans, but they flocked to British Malaya to start a new life under the protection of the Crown. Most were escaping extreme poverty and political repression back home: some came to Malaya as scratch-in-the-dirt day labourers while others came as craftsmen, and still others saw the opportunity to move their family wealth far from the Celestial Emperor; some came as plantation labour, and through hard work, luck and what they themselves termed as 'being clever' had managed to save enough to invest and eventually rise to prominence.

Grandfather Low, the son of the successful owners of a roadside vegetable stall, had come from Shantou. He had invested family money in a pineapple plantation near Jelita in the early days of colonial Singapore. Once that operation had proven itself profitable, he had bought over the pineapple processing and tinning operations. And once that became profitable as well, he had turned his attention to the tin found in the Klang Valley of Selangor. He had bought a mine and smelting operation, which he then placed in the care of his brother, and, together, they manufactured the tins into which Low's pineapples would be packed and sold. Soon, another brother was brought over from

China and employed. More land was bought. More mines were acquired. Connections were made with Teochew families in Siam and Borneo. Secret societies were formed; more companies were opened; more brothers and cousins became employed. When Grandfather Low finally got around to having a son of his own, he was on the verge of starting his own shipping company. Why should he pay other people to transport his tins of pineapple to Australia, or his tropical timber to Japan, or his Sarawak pepper to the world?

When Low Hun Chiu, his first child and only son was born, he was destined to become the scion and de-facto head of a dynastic empire that stretched from Bangkok to Kuching. It was involved in every form of legitimate trade and manufacture that could be found in the lands around the South China Sea. Dozens of companies would be under his control, many in places he would never visit. He would also be destined to become the *kapitan* of the Low *kongsi*, which stretched its nefarious influence not only across the South Sea but all the way back home to Guangdong Province.

'The laws of humanity are temporary things,' Grandfather Low guided his son. 'Our duty is to the family, to the keeping of health, the gaining of wisdom and the increasing of wealth. That is the way to prosperity. The British make laws just as the Emperor makes laws just. And we must obey these laws with one face while making our own laws with our own family and brothers. We will have one face for the British. We will pay their duties and show our obedience and raise ourselves in their legal trade. We will have another face for our Chinese brothers, who know and respect our way of life.'

In practice, the Low Empire had two sets of books, though in actual application, the two entities piggy-backed each other, and it was often hard to see where one ended and the other began. Grandfather Low stocked the coolie labour force on his legally owned plantations through a network of illegal human traffickers, who were known to be extremely brutal, but whom he deftly managed to control. He supplied opium to the rickshaw pullers, and he supplied tinned fruit to the governor's wife. His *kongsi* openly contended with the Cantonese and the Hokkien for control of the lucrative British-administered license concessions known as 'farms' for opium and alcohol and tobacco and valuables, and also fought violently for the control of the parallel black market trade in these same commodities.

In Hawksworth's day, Grandfather Low had decided to build a stately home in the suburban enclave of River Valley Road, with a commanding view of the same river from which so much wealth had flowed to him. For the family seat, he had chosen a site near Killiney Road, on land that was rumoured to be the burial ground of a naval officer who had been in the service of the Sultan of Singapore. Subsequently, the estate came to be called Panglima Prang, Malay for 'war admiral' and a suitable epithet for the home of a raider in the commercial and non-commercial trades of the day. The property stretched all the way down to the river, so that a stroll would bring one to the very backs of the family controlled godowns, the tops of which were visible from the lawn of the house.

The rickshaw puller, huffing and puffing after the exertion of bringing Hawksworth up the steep incline that led to the house, dropped his charge and indicated that he would wait by the front gate, which was shielded from view by a wall of tall hedges.

The Chief Detective Inspector had not been to the house in a number of years, and as he approached it now, the oddity of the architecture, for which the building was justifiably notorious, struck him anew. The floor plan of Panglima Prang followed that of a traditional tropical bungalow; however, the floor was the only traditional aspect of the house's architecture. Grandfather Low had wrapped his house with a veranda planted with oversized Doric columns so that the outer walls had the appearance of Roman baths. To complete the oddity, a green-tiled Chinese roof projected over the house so that the whole resembled the architectural equivalent of a rummage sale, as though it had been assembled from spare parts. It was said that there was no other house in the East quite like it.

From his previous visits, the tall man knew that the interiors of the house would continue with this mishmash display of the Orient and the Occident. As he entered, waiting in the foyer while the servant who opened the door fetched the family, he was faced with an airy central room filled with rosewood furniture in-laid with mother-of-pearl motifs in high chinoiserie. Portraits of Low ancestors, going back several generations, glared down at overstuffed Victorian sofas and chairs that lay strewn among the Oriental hardwood.

After an interminable time in the hot, buzzing quiet of the foyer, he was led into an adjacent room that was fitted out as a reception and meeting area, also decorated with a jumbled mix of furniture. A gilt mirror hung over a raised dais, which acted as the seating area where the family would sit when receiving guests. Hawksworth observed that the mirror was angled up slightly so that it could catch the light of a grand crystal chandelier; at night, it would reflect the chandelier's light in dazzling patterns, bouncing it all over the furniture, causing one's mind to reel as if under the unpleasant influence of bad champagne.

The servant all but shoved Hawksworth into a chair facing the dais, where sat three scowling Chinese faces. The Lows did not take kindly to police detectives barging in unannounced, especially immediately after breakfast.

Low Hun Chiu, whose lustrous black queue was tipped with red silk down to his heels, had two sons of nearly equal age, both of whom he detested. He was purposefully leaving his line of succession vague so that neither one would become presumptuous while the old man was alive, and he thought that it would be best for the boys to fight for the leadership position once he had joined his ancestors. In their current duties, each had control of one of the two wings – one of the legitimate business and the other of the illicit variety – of the family empire.

Nonetheless, whenever important business needed to be transacted, both were present, as they were now, sitting quietly on either side of their father. Hawksworth could never remember which one was named what, though he knew their faces and their assigned roles. One was fat and vicious, with a thug's dumpling face. Smug and assured in manner, he obviously enjoyed applying the hot blade to naked skin when the time called for it. He was dressed in the accustomed manner of the well-to-do Chinese merchant, in loose trousers and a high-collared, heavy-buttoned tunic, in solid colours and of very fine cotton. Like his father's, his hair was worn in a queue, with the front of his head shaved and the long pigtail dangling behind him. Unlike this father, there was no red silk braided into his hair.

The other brother was thin and tall, with a pinched, deviously intelligent face. He wore Western clothing, trousers and a shirt with oyster shell buttons, along with a silk tie. His hair was cropped short and parted in the middle, and pomaded closely to his scalp so that his head looked shellacked. To those who knew China, it was clear that he would never return to the land of the Emperor. He also wore glasses, and he spoke fluent English with the slight Oxbridge accent of the upper class he was raised to penetrate. He would act as interpreter for his family.

The room was silent except for the swish of the cloth overhead, pulled by the punkah boy. The fat one watched Hawksworth with the expression of a dog licking its chops; the thin one had glittering black rat's eyes that never left the detective's face. Hawksworth leaned slightly forward and addressed the elder Low directly in English: 'Thank you for seeing me today, Low Hun Chiu.' In another few years, Hawksworth would have to add the honorific Malay title of 'Dato' to the man's name, but for now the semi-royal status of the businessman was implied only by his being seated slightly above his guest.

The Teochew talk flowed, and as always the Chief Detective Inspector was impressed by the sing-song quality of the language. To his ear, it sounded like a polished version of Hokkien, the stresses less angular, the vowel sounds more refined. There was an ancient animosity between the two groups, with the Teochew looking down on the Hokkien as lesser members of the same family, like rude country cousins. Hawksworth wondered if this attitude had some reflection in their language.

The elder Low spoke in deep but melodious tones, still staring directly at Hawksworth while the thin son beside him translated his Teochew words.

'Chief Detective Inspector Hawksworth is always most welcome in this house. The great service he performed for the temple society in apprehending the man who defaced our ancestor's tomb is one that can never be repaid.'

The case of the missing headstone was not one of which Hawksworth was proud. Yong Seng had stolen the heavy stone from the bathtub-like grave of Grandfather Low when the Mother-Flower clan had been in a territorial battle with the Lows over the control of a strip of contested godowns closest to the river's mouth. When the negotiations were concluded, and it had been time to return the massive piece of stonework, Hawksworth was tasked with the duty. Recognising that it would create good feelings all around – and positive press for the Detective Branch – he had complied. Despite the fact that the Lows then swore a blood-oath of revenge on the Mother-Flowers, everyone maintained the myth that Hawksworth had somehow uncovered a great mystery and heroically restored the object to its rightful owners. It was smoother for business to behave in such a way.

'The humble pleasure I took in returning such an important piece to a family of such high respect is something that I continue to experience. I hope that someday I may again perform such a service for the Low family, though under less unfortunate circumstances.'

'It is with utmost gratitude that we continue our profound respect for the police department and especially for the Detective Branch, of which we were inestimably pleased to learn that our dear Detective Inspector Hawksworth was made Chief.'

'I thank you, and I say to you that so long as I remain in such capacity in Her Majesty's service, I will do my utmost to ensure that the Low family is always correctly protected and rewarded for their on-going civic efforts to Singapore.'

'Thank you, Chief Detective Inspector.' A tea service was placed on the table beside the detective's chair, though he dared not touch it until the elder Low had drunk from his own steaming cup. 'We are always glad to have you visit our home, but surely today's visit is not merely of a social nature?'

'Unfortunately, you are correct. I am here today on official police business. Two days ago we recovered the body of a white man from Rochor Canal. We believe that he was an American involved in the ice trade. As the Rochor Canal District is part of Mr. Low's ...' he searched for the polite word, 'enclave, I am hoping that he has some knowledge of this unfortunate incident.'

Again, there was a flow of Teochew words, and then the thin son asked indifferently, 'How can we be of assistance to you in this matter?'

'I stress that I do not believe that the Low family is in any way implicated in the death of this stranger, but only that, perhaps, through your business establishments, you have heard more than I have. The death of a foreigner in such a manner must be taken seriously by the police.' And he immediately regretted this tack, for the implication of his words could be that Low did not take such matters seriously when they occurred within his own estate, that he was a poor manager of his own territory.

The old man did not change expression, however, but spoke to his sons for a long while. His thin son translated: 'We aware of the importance of the death, but we know little more than the police. It is always possible that the body drifted along the canal, for there was no violent action in our businesses in that district …' the son paused as he sought a delicate phrase, 'and we had no business with this white man, and if we did, upon hearing of his death, we would have wanted to, without hesitation, seek the kind advice of our friends in the police.'

It seemed that the elder Low was being sympathetic today, for he had given Hawksworth a chance to redeem the face he had inadvertently lost. 'The Low's family business practices are known to be impeccable and beyond reproach, and the families continued cooperation with the police and business community is greatly appreciated at the highest levels of Her Majesty's government in Singapore. Let us say no more on this matter.'

After he had heard the interpretation, the elder Low's face muscles eased into a slight smile. 'Would the Chief Detective Inspector perhaps care for some tea?'

'Yes, thank you. That would be lovely.'

The son said, 'Low Hun Chiu,' for the elder Low was never addressed as 'my father' by his sons to a third party in the father's presence, 'was interested to learn that a ship had docked the day previous to the discovery of the body in Rochor Canal. A native ship, from Batavia. This ship later burned.'

'I am aware of that ship, and I am also aware that the ship burnt. I also believe that the dead American is connected to that near-catastrophe. In fact,' Hawksworth decided it was time to press the issue, 'with all due respect, I happened to be there when it burnt down; I was investigating information that opium was being smuggled into Singapore from that ship. And furthermore,' the Chief Detective Inspector looked directly at the floor near the elder Low's feet, 'I was told that the illicit opium was being smuggled on behalf of the Low *kongsi*.'

All three faces before him remained impassive. The fact that the Low *kongsi* was involved with smuggling opium was no secret. How the Chief Detective Inspector had come to hear of such specifics of their trade – which ship they had used, and at which time and at which wharf – had piqued their interest, but they knew that asking him about this directly would get them nowhere. Instead, and this was implicitly understood, they would make their own inquiries with the spies and leaks in their organisation. And Hawksworth would now be watched very closely. A Western face would have betrayed outrage at such an accusation, but the Oriental faces arrayed before him simply waited for the next card to turn. After a lifetime in Malaya, Hawksworth was prepared for this wall of Chinese silence.

'And I believe that the death of the American is directly related to the opium smuggling, and I have every intention of making the matter public. Murder and arson are serious crimes,' he said archly, adding under his breath, 'even in Singapore.'

This time the family conferred with each other in rapid fire

Teochew; the fat son quickly became animated, remonstrating with the thin son, then directly with his father. Finally the elder Low raised his hand, palm up, and the fat son, red-faced, shut up. Clearing his throat, the thin son said, 'As loyal subjects of the Crown Colony of Singapore, we want to assist your investigation in every way possible. However, we are afraid that you are mistaken in one important point. Yes, the ship was to be used to smuggle opium, but the opium was to be transhipped from Singapore to Java. It did not bring any opium – as far as we know – into Singapore,' he announced, pronouncing the final word as *thing-ah-poor*.

This piece of information caught the Chief Detective Inspector off-guard, but he remained composed. 'And you know nothing of the American? Or of the ship burning?'

The fat son glared sullenly as his thin brother very carefully explained, 'Like you, we believe the American entered Singapore on the same ship. Our people saw a white man leave the vessel and thought this was odd. How or why he was killed, we do not know. The burning of the ship was of great inconvenience to us, and we are looking into the matter ourselves. But as you know, the Beach Road quay is mostly controlled by Hakka, and they are not always to be trusted.'

Hawksworth sighed, sipped his tea until the cup was empty, and then replaced it with a clatter. 'Then we know only as much as the other?'

There was another brief exchange, this time between the elder Low and the thin son only. The latter finally said, 'No, we also have information about the ship on the night before it was burnt.'

'I am listening.'

'Although the ship came in from Batavia, the crew spoke Kling and met a party when the ship arrived.'

'Yes?'

'Late at night, they returned to the ship – without the American – and off-loaded cargo in the dark.'

'Go on.'

'It seems that the cargo was about the size and shape of a child, though very heavy, for it took three men to lift it and load it onto a bullock cart. One of our men attempted to follow this cart, but he was unable to keep track of it. Klings can be difficult to see at night.'

'Klings?'

The elder Low now answered, in a rumbling voice for emphasis, directly to Hawksworth: 'Klings.'

Hawksworth knew his audience with the Low family was now short, but he asked two more questions, quickly in succession: 'Was the cargo alive?'

The thin son answered, 'It did not appear to be moving, and it was too heavy to have been a man. Or an animal.'

'What else on earth would an American smuggle into Singapore?'

After the thin son had translated this for his family, the fat son said jovially, in very heavily accented English. 'Wah! Maybe he bringing ice.'

The elder Low now rose, with Hawksworth and his sons following him. The two elder men thanked each other for the visit, the pleasure of the conversation, the honour of seeing one another again. Before they parted, the elder Low said in perfectly clear English: 'Who smuggles ice? You cannot make money that way.' Then he chortled the Chinese chortle that denotes personal amusement at the obvious stupidity of an inferior.

CHAPTER VI

The Boustead Institute
for Seamen

HAWKSWORTH STOOD GAZING up at portrait of Edward Boustead. On the other side of the room, an aged sailor hammered away at the ivory keys of a poorly tuned upright piano. The sailor sang along loudly, his voice just as raspy and off key as his piano.

'Eternal Father, strong to save
whose arm hath bound the restless wave.
Who biddest the mighty ocean deep
its own appointed limits keep.'

'As I am sure you are aware, Chief Detective Inspector, one of Mr. Boustead's last wishes was for the construction of a home for sailors. This building is the realisation of his dream,' said Alastair Stewart, standing beside Hawksworth, also looking up at the portrait of Edward Boustead. A new arrival in the colony from the Boustead office in London, he was Managing Director of the large network of companies that Boustead and Company had created in the six decades since Edward Boustead had first set foot in Singapore. He was of medium build, with a ruddy face and a head of thick grey hair; he looked roughly Hawksworth's age, perhaps a few years older.

The office in the warehouse across from Clark Quay was currently undergoing renovations, so the top management of the company were working, for the time being, out of the Boustead Institute, which had been built recently on Tanjong Pagar Road as a rest and way station for infirm sailors.

'But that is not all. He also gave generously to the hospital for sailors and to the Cathedral of the Good Shepherd.' He spoke with a froggy, constricted voice, as if someone were strangling him. The Scots lilt was covered with a patina of English public school, and the mix was not entirely pleasant to the ear.

'Most Holy Spirit! Who didst brood
upon the chaos dark and rude,
and bid its angry tumult cease
and give, for wild confusion, peace.'

The sailor's rough voice filled the spaces between the poorly tuned notes, which rattled around the room like clacking bones.

'Mr. Boustead was truly concerned with the future prosperity of Singapore. ' Stewart pronounced the name as *sing-UH-pour*.

'I am aware of the contribution Mr. Boustead made to the colony.' Much like the Lows, Boustead had made a point of getting his fingers into very possible pie in Singapore. And as a means of gaining access to society, once he could afford it, the Yorkshireman had spent lavishly on civic works. He was also the person who first brought the Hong Kong and Shanghai Banking Corporation to Singapore, and in his capacity as sole agent, he could loan money to his own interests at cheap rates while starving his competitors.

'He was also very much involved with the local Chinese and Kling business associations, as we still are to this day. Indeed, we are currently working with one of our long-standing Kling associates in the banking trade, Mr. Chettiar, to raise money to build a grand Hindu temple near the canal where the dhobis wash clothing. A great new century is nearly upon us – one in which all God's children shall live in harmony.'

'O Trinity of love and power
our brethren shield in danger's hour
From rock and tempest, fire and foe
Protect them wheresoever they go.'

'My understanding is that Boustead also owns the Singapore Ice Company?'

'We do; the business was started some years ago when the chemical production of ice became a cheaper prospect than importing it all the way from America.'

'So you now never import ice?'

'Yes, we do very occasionally, but only when local production is expected to fall short. We took over the contract from a Chinese firm when they decided the profits were too small. For that matter, I cannot recall the last time Boustead brought any ice into Singapore. The icehouse on the river near the Assembly Rooms is still ours as well, though we distribute through our own firm these days. I believe that we rent out the space in the old icehouse for warehousing.'

'What is the name of the American company with which you do business?'

'I believe that it is called the Neptune Ice Company.'

'And were you expecting any shipments recently?'

'No. In fact we frequently overproduce ice in our own facility.'

'Were you expecting any company agents to arrive in the past few days?'

'From Neptune? No, not at all. What is all this about, Chief Detective Inspector?'

Hawksworth frowned. 'The corpse of a white man, whom we believe to be American, was pulled from Rochor Canal two days ago.'

Stewart paused purposefully – and Hawksworth noted this – then assumed a look that blended concern with repulsion. 'A corpse? How terrible.'

'Oh hear us when we cry to thee
for those in peril on the sea.'

'In his rooms we found his calling card. It stated that he worked for the Neptune Ice Company. We believe he might have been involved in a smuggling operation.'

Hawksworth watched as the man's face changed from feigned

horror and concern to one of bafflement. 'Surely you are not suggesting that Boustead and Company or any of our subsidiary companies had anything to do with this unfortunate affair?'

'No, of course not. But I thought perhaps you were aware of this man's presence in Singapore.'

'As I said, we were not expecting any agents from Neptune, or any other ice importation company, for that matter.'

'Thus evermore shall rise to Thee
Glad hymns of praise from land and sea.'

The sailor at the piano stopped playing, though the sound of his hoarse voice continued to linger ghost-like in the room. 'Thank you for your time, Mr. Stewart. If there is any more information you believe would be of use to me, please let me know.'

'Good day to you, Chief Detective Inspector.'

The two men turned away from the portrait and began to walk in opposite directions. Suddenly Stewart stopped to ask, 'What is it you think he might have been smuggling?'

The tall man straightened his shoulders, 'We do not know. Perhaps opium, perhaps people, perhaps timber, perhaps ... ice.'

A croaking laugh burst forth from the red-faced man, but quickly collapsed into an apology delivered in a choked voice. 'I am sorry, Chief Detective Inspector. I can understand the smuggling of opium, but not of ice. Who would bother to smuggle ice?'

'That is exactly what I plan on finding out, Mr. Stewart. That is it exactly.'

Much like the icehouse on the river, Hawksworth noticed for the first time as he walked away from it, the Boustead Institute was a wedge-shaped building. Three stories tall, ornamented in a neo-classical style with a large clock on the prominent crest of the building's prow, its resemblance to a ship was no accident. It had been built into the top of an X-shaped intersection, at the junction of Tanjong Pagar Road and Anson Road, along the main route from New Harbour into town. The same tram tracks that ran past Hawksworth's office in the Central Police Station brought the smoking, clanging tram cars past the windows of the convalescent sailors. At the opposite corner of the X was the Tanjong Pagar police station, with its distinctive circular shape and cupola.

The afternoon sun was glazing the sky a bright white. Nothing moved in the shimmering heat at the centre of the X-intersection: for the moment, it was as if Hawksworth had stepped onto a brightly lit stage set, without shadows. A light breeze stirred the red dust of the road. In the far horizon, cumulous clouds were massing above the Riau Islands, too far away to promise rain.

Hawksworth moved through the eerie heat and silence, towards an embankment on the right. Carts and rickshaws began to appear at the far stretches of the roads, heading towards the centre of the junction, and towards the tall man who stood at the centre of the X, sweat pouring down the runnel of his back, in the meagre shade of the few trees he found planted outside a bungalow.

He hailed a passing rickshaw, pulling the heavy canvas shade against the blinding afternoon sunshine. He looked at the sweat and grime on the narrow dark shoulders of the wallah, at his taut muscles jerking in the blazing heat as he ran.

As his sweaty body slipped down against the warm leather of the rickshaw seat, he mused about the question Stewart had just asked him: Who smuggles ice, indeed?

* * *

The *angsana* blooms were long gone, the branches of the trees drooping in the heat of the seemingly endless drought.

From his office window, where he was leaning out to catch the slight breeze that signalled the onset of evening, Hawksworth watched the traffic pass by on the street below. A patrol of four Sikh policemen, attired in their khaki shorts and soft brown boots, led by a grim-faced British Army officer in a jaunty white-peaked cork topee, marched along South Bridge Road towards the river, raising a cloud of red dust.

The Sikhs were a fearsome presence in the colony. They served a paramilitary function, somewhere between the police and the army: they were shock troops, ordered to keep the natives in line. The Chinese feared the Sikhs as though they were monsters, and to their minds the Sikhs – thick-set, fierce-faced hairy men with striped red and white turbans, flinty eyes and flaring nostrils – resembled the traditional Chinese depiction of demons. They had even begun to place plaster statues of Sikh officers as sentinels at their doorways and beside graves, along with the more traditional effigies of lions and dragons, to frighten away evil spirits.

The Malays were less impressed with the Sikhs. They called them *kepala udang*, or 'prawn heads,' or in other words, 'shit for brains'. As the contingent went on with their marching, Hawksworth observed that there was indeed something prawnish about their movement, with their arms swinging and their stripped turbans turning this way and that, and the barrels of their carbines slung over their arms, protruding like antenna.

His door creaked open and Rizby entered, treading across the bare floorboards. Turning from the window, Hawksworth sat in his desk chair and motioned for the shorter man to sit. The taller man sighed deeply.

'Any progress, sir?'

'Not really. I only have a great amalgamation of facts that makes little sense. What have you learned?'

'There is still no sign of the crew of that burnt ship.'

'Of course, not. They simply melted into the crowd. Low Hun Chiu told me that the crew were Klings. Rather improbable for a vessel sailing from Java.'

'Klings, sir?'

Hawksworth cocked his eyebrow, then said, 'I will tell you a fact, and you will tell me another.'

This was a game the two detectives played, which they called, for reasons now forgotten, 'beggar the police'.

'A white man was found dead and nude in Rochor Canal.'

'White men of a certain station do not wash up dead in canals. They die in their beds.'

'There were no signs of violence or struggle except for a bump on his head.' 'He was unconscious when he went into the water.'

'So the water killed him. He drowned.'

'But he was nude, thus evidence of his identity was deliberately removed. This cannot be a petty crime.'

'The white man was murdered.'

'Yes. And not by Chinese gangs as there was no mutilation.'

'Subsequently, we found evidence to suggest that the white man was an American who worked for the Neptune Ice Company.'

'Did any ice come into Singapore recently?'

'No, and the new manager at Boustead told me that no shipments of ice were expected from the Neptune Ice Company.'

'And a ship, which we believe he used to enter the island, was subsequently burnt in a very public manner.'

'Again hiding evidence. And committing murder.'

'To silence the captain.'

'The crew disappeared.'

'So are they complicit?'

'Or they were bought off. Or they, too, will also start turning up dead.'

'And finally there is the matter of the mysterious cargo the dead white man supposedly smuggled into the colony. Accompanied by Klings.'

'Any indication of what it was?'

'Low told me that it was too large to be opium and too heavy to be a man.'

'And Americans are known to smuggle men, opium, and—'

'Ice?' Hawksworth cut in.

'Ice? Who smuggles ice?' Rizby asked quizzically.

Silence.

'To begin again: we have a dead American. A dead ship captain. An incinerated ship. We have witnesses who said they saw the dead man smuggle something hidden under a tarp. With Kling accomplices. On a ship that would burn to the waterline less than twenty-four hours later.'

'The men were murdered, and the ship was burnt to hide evidence of the smuggling.'

'And what, pray tell, could possibly be so important to smuggle that it would require the killing of two men and the public burning of a ship to remove evidence?'

'Weapons? Guns?'

'That is a disturbing possibility. But gun smugglers do not tend to attract attention to themselves with wild acts of arson.'

'What about suspects?'

'Suspects? They abound! The Lows. The new managing director of Boustead and Company. Everyone associated with that dead American is wealthy and connected to powerful interests.'

'Why would any of them import arms?'

Silence.

Rizby said, 'Perhaps for transhipment?'

'Perhaps.'

'Which brings us back to the only other possibility: ice.'

'Smuggling ice, and then killing for it? That is simply daft.'

There was silence, filled only with a hawker's cry in Tamil from the street below. Their 'beggar the police' game was over. Hawksworth began drumming his fingers on his desk. With the sun setting outside, the office was getting dark.

'I think I should pay another visit to my friends at the Mother-

Flower *kongsi*.'

'Should I go with you, sir?'

'There is no need of that, Detective Inspector. Good evening.'

'Good evening, sir.'

As Hawksworth rose up behind his desk, Rizby got to his feet as well. The Chief Detective Inspector muttered, 'I do not like ice, Rizby. It does not belong here. The Americans perverted nature when they first brought it here. Ice has no place in the tropics.'

'There was an incident between you and a lady at the icehouse, when you were in Madras, was there not, sir?'

Hawksworth glowered at the little fox-faced man.

'I am sorry, Chief Detective Inspector, I did not mean to ...' Rizby, normally fleet of tongue, found himself stumbling for words.

Turning back to the window, where the long shadows were playing across the gingerbread facade of the Police Court across the street, Hawksworth sighed. 'Yes, it was at the icehouse in Madras that ...' He paused as the memories of the humiliation came painfully to his mind. 'Good night, Detective Inspector.'

'Good night, sir.'

* * *

Almeida Street was raucous by night. Laughing men strolled along the five-foot-way in small groups, some spilling out into the dimly lit street, the moon bright above, casting blue shadows on white and yellow faces already purple with drink. Sounds of music and louder laughter came from the orange windows on the second and third floors of the shophouses. The smells of vegetables frying in oyster sauce, of rice boiling and of pork fat grilling on charcoal braziers mingled with the effluence of alcohol and tobacco, with the heavy dark perfume of opium. Running through this potpourri were the brassy odours of acrid male sweat and of hot bullock dung squashed into the dirt of the street.

The half-gate doorway of the Mother-Flower house was blocked by a man who stood almost as wide as the entrance. Considering the man's size, Hawksworth grew certain that the *kongsi* brothers were expecting trouble to turn up on their own doorstep. At Hawksworth's approach, the man merely raised his hand, palm outward, to stop the taller man. The detective beat out a quick hello in Hokkien then simply said 'Yong Seng'.

Loudly, the guard barked the same name into the noise of the ground floor room, and moments later Yong Seng was there, hustling the Chief Detective Inspector into the house. Yong Seng already stank of rice wine and strong tobacco, and moved with a stumbling gait as he ascended the stairs.

Upstairs, Yong Chern still laid sprawled upright in his great fatness on the rosewood sofa, a black cheroot blazing in his hand. Only now his shiny black pigtail was plaited neatly behind him, one end curled around his neck, and he was resplendent in a fine silk vest and a black *changshan* patterned with darker black designs. The beatific look on his face remained unchanged when Yong Seng and Hawksworth walked in.

He immediately noticed the same sprite-like girl he had seen before, still seated on the floor, the bhang pipe between her doll-like legs. Shu En was now attired in a tight-fitting one-piece smock with a mandarin collar, coloured corn-silk blue and with light floral patterns on the flared edges of the sleeves. Her hair was plaited tightly behind her head and coiled into a bun, with a few wispy strays falling onto her forehead and over her thin neck, sticking to her flesh in the damp heat, tracing black lines like tattoos on her moonshine skin. She looked up at the Chief Detective Inspector, ejected a thin line of smoke from her coral lips, then smiled and greeted him softly in Hokkien.

'Chief Detective Inspector Hawksworth. What brings our very good friend back to our humble house so soon?' Yong Chern said in rumbling English, his eyes opening a little wider.

'Good evening, Chong Yong Chern. I have come here to enjoy your company, of course. My recent visit to your house only reminded me of how much I relish our time together.'

Yong Chern smiled and gestured to the chair beside the small inlaid table. 'Please sit, Chief Detective Inspector. Your flattery betrays dissatisfaction.'

The sudden silence in the room was punctuated by a rough shout from downstairs. A scuffle could be heard through the floorboards; someone evidently did not like the way their dice game was going. Yong Seng quickly bowed out to attend to the problem.

'Yes, unfortunately,' Hawksworth continued, 'the information you so graciously gave me proved to be incorrect. You see, the opium was not being smuggled by the Lows into Singapore. It was being smuggled out of Singapore, into Java.'

Yong Chern laughed the edged Chinese laugh that indicated discomfort and a slight loss of face, but the laugh also meant that the conversation – and their friendship – was in no jeopardy. 'Your contacts are better than our own, I see! Perhaps you are the biggest dog of the big dogs?' and he laughed the raucous Chinese laugh that meant touché among friends when face was at stake.

The banter worked, and Hawksworth relaxed. 'Did you know that the ship burnt down?'

'Yes, I heard.'

'Any idea why someone would want to burn it?'

He shook his head.

'Then I do not suppose you have any idea who burnt it?'

Again, Yong Chern shook his head.

Hawksworth sighed then slumped forward, his elbows pressed into the dark wood of the table top, 'Why do you have the orang-utan at the front door? Expecting trouble?'

Yong Chern laughed a mirthful laugh. 'Orang-utan! Very funny! In Malay the words mean—'

'Yes, I know what they mean. Who is that large fellow?'

'That is Cheang Sam Teo.'

'He looks as if he could tear a man apart with his bare hands.'

'We call him "monster," but "orang-utan" sounds better!'

'Why do you need a monster at your front door?' Yong Chern said, 'We have news. Yap Sew Heng, the *kapitan* of Hai San *kongsi*, is now allied with the Lows. At the next auction of the opium and spirit farm, the Low and Hai San will come together to control both. Instead of fighting, they are going to join forces.'

'You have spoken before of this joint monopoly. So now the Lows and Hai San will dominate the liquor and opium trades, both legal and illegal.'

Yong Chern shrugged. 'The Mother-Flowers and the other Hokkien *kongsi* will not allow this. We will fight the Lows and the Hai San combined, if we must.'

'You intend to take on both the Teochew and the Cantonese clans?' Hawksworth considered the bloodbath that would ensue: the violence would be quickly followed by the heavy-handed reprisal of the colonial authorities. It would be a vicious little war, but not one that would make the London – or even the Calcutta – newspapers.

'Yes, if we must.'

'What do you intend to do? Steal their gravestones again?' the Chief Detective Inspector said sarcastically.

'A true magician never uses the same trick twice,' Yong Chern said in all seriousness. 'Now, my very good friend, I cannot discuss this matter with you any further. If you would like to stay here and enjoy our company, you are welcome to do so.'

'Otherwise, I should sod off': The words remained unspoken, though the meaning was clear.

'A few sips of wine before I head home, thank you.'

A dark bottle of rice wine and some heavy glasses were brought into the room. The liquid was hot and burnt his throat as it slipped down his gullet, but then, quickly, came the relaxing of his nerves and the intensification of the senses that the tall man had come to expect. Hawksworth had a few more sips and stared at the glowing end of Yong Chern's cheroot while the heavy man stroked the jet-black hair of the pale girl. They stayed quiet, sipping the wine, listening to the noises of the house, slipping further into a haze of leisurely contemplation. The bottle was quickly drained, and another was brought in its place. A young man appeared before them with a *zhongruan*, the circular resonator painted like a full moon, which he began to strum while singing softly in Hokkien.

The pixie-faced girl suddenly rose to her feet. She deftly carried the water pipe to the table, and slipped the end of its tube between Hawksworth's lips. Her tiny coral mouth smiled – no words came out of it – as he took a deep drag of the bhang. Yong Chern let loose his ox laugh while the detective exhaled a cloud of thick blue smoke. The girl murmured something in Hokkien, and the fat man said a few words in return. Hawksworth was only inches away from the smooth moonglow skin of Shu En's face, from the narrow dark eyes that were looking into his own. The girl murmured again: he realised that she was describing to Yong Chern what she was seeing as she inspected Hawksworth, his pointed nose, his chest hairs protruding from his shirt, his lactic odour. But the big Chinese man was not paying attention: his eyes were closed, his head lolling to the music.

Hawksworth sat immobilised, as if he were sitting on his hands, while the girl crept even closer, slipped her small nose against his cheek and inhaled, giving him an Oriental kiss. He was staring at the white skin behind her tiny ear, at each jet black strand growing from there, each black hair perfectly visible as it emerged from her pale flesh, so that he could count each one. Then he smelled the delightful spot behind her ear where the roots of the hair were growing. It was reminiscent of winter melon, a sweet, clean, moist smell, almost crisp. He moved his nose closer while she slid onto his lap. She unbuttoned his cuff and rolled up his sleeve to examine the hairs on his arm. She plucked at them, fascinated. His left hand crept up, towards a smooth cheek.

The spell was broken when Yong Seng entered the room suddenly, without knocking. The musician stopped abruptly; the party noise from the downstairs room now filled the small room. The girl looked at Yong Seng with finely narrowed eyes; Yong Chern's eyes popped open. The two men exchanged fast and loud Hokkien, which Hawksworth could not follow.

'My dear Chief Detective Inspector, I am afraid that we have some immediate business that needs our attention elsewhere. You are welcome to stay here until we return,' he said, then beginning to appreciate the situation in the room. 'Shu En will see to your needs,' he said. Then the two men left.

The girl looked at Yong Chern when she heard her name embedded within his sentence of English words. Then she turned to Hawksworth, a mischievous smile on her coral lips. She was lovely and he was tempted indeed, but Hawksworth had a woman at home – which was at least three quarters of an hour away by hackney carriage. Tonight would not be the night for exploring the delightful wonders Shu En's smiling face promised. He moved the girl off him and then stood on unsteady legs.

His mind afloat in a cloud of rice wine and bhang smoke, he made his light-footed way through the dry dirt and deep pools of shadow of the noisy street. A passing fruit vendor sold him a pineapple slice skewered on a stick. A constable in uniform, whom he did not recognise, saluted him on the corner. Hawksworth hoped that his bloodshot eyes were hidden from the subordinate by the darkness.

He walked to the hackney carriage station on New Bridge Road, crawled into a sweltering box, sprawled himself across one of the sticky leather seats, then watched the red lanterns swaying bright and crazy in the darkness outside the windows as the horses' hooves clopped a lulling rhythm.

By the time they reached his bungalow, set amidst the swaying palms of Geylang, he was fast asleep in the seat, dreaming of the icehouse in Madras, shining like a sunlit temple on the Coromandel Coast.

CHAPTER VII

Stone Water

THE RAIN FINALLY came on Laylat al-Qadr, the 'Night of Power' that marks the beginning of the last ten days of Ramadan. As though it were making up for lost time, the water fell in torrents, turning the sky the colour of a bruise. The streets that had been parched became puddles, then ponds. Red laterite mud clung to everything it touched, hooves, boots, wheels, toes; tracked indoors, it infested the spaces under desks and tables, stuck in the nooks behind bookcases, stained the wainscoting of European homes. By the time it was Hari Raya Aidilfitri, the closing feast of the holy month, it seemed as if the island was half-sunk, covered in treacherous blood-red mud.

Hawksworth sat at his desk reading aloud an open letter to His Excellency the Governor, apparently penned by a rickshaw puller, then printed in *The Straits Times*:

MOST POWERFUL SIR, Permit thy humble servant to approach thee by the way of my friend, Tan Tan Tiam, who knoweth the Ang Moh's speech, and kindly consenteth to write to him who moveth the Government to influence the Tye Jin to have compassion upon the exiled sons of China.

Thy servant is a humble puller of the man-power-carriage by night, and is suffering grievously because he is unable to carry on his lawful occupation of plying by hire, by reason of the dire fear that besetteth him. It hath come to the ears of thy servant and of his fellows, that the Ang Moh's engineers do seek a sacrifice to appease the offended gods of Earth and Water, whom they have outraged by disturbing his habitation on the hill that standeth behind the office of the Tye Jin, which they of India call Ko-mis-a-yat. The said engineers, perchance from ignorance, have neglected to consult the wise ones of earth-lore as to the means to be taken to please the said spirits, who have consequently so tormented the Ang Moh that they seek a sacrifice. Not of the rich and family-blessed, who would make a complaint to the Government, if they were sacrificed, but of us poor and friendless man-power carriage coolies, who in the exercise of our nightly avocation are called to distant parts of the town, where the knife that is invisible will speedily sever the head from the body, and the cloth that is impenetrable will stifle the last cry of him that hath none to avenge, and our heads go to make the water run within the pipe, and make firm the foundations of this new water hole.

Let the engineers make the necessary sacrifices, so that we may go without fear and trembling to those who call us, with mighty voice and thick, to go to Si Poi Poh. Then shall we receive the reward of the Ang Moh's gratitude, far exceeding that of they who aforetime dwelt in the land, or of our brothers of the Celestial Empire.

Signed, HAK-CHEW

It was another head-cutting scare, this time relating to the municipal waterworks and the laying of pipes. The first of these scares happened back in the 1860s during the construction of St. Andrew's Church. Not long after the church had been completed, its steeple had been struck by lightning. Consequently, the building was declared unsound until proper engineering inspections could be carried out. In the meantime, the Anglican Community was forced to attend services in the Court House.

This change of venue led some Chinese to believe that the Europeans had abandoned the church because of the presence of evil spirits, which the labourers had unknowingly unleashed upon the structure while breaking open the ground for laying its foundations. Therefore, in order to appease these demonic spirits, it was suggested that the Europeans offer thirty human heads as sacrifice; these heads, it was also suggested, could be claimed from either the community of convicts or of hapless rickshaw drivers – the poor would not be missed, after all.

In response, the working convicts (as with most municipal buildings and roads and infrastructure in Singapore, the church had been built by the hands of native convict labour) called a general strike, which mostly meant that they stayed in their squalid quarters broiling all day long while the guards sat in the shades of the palms in the courtyard drinking arrack. Finally, it was reasoned that the only way to cajole everyone into working again was to have the community leaders explain the situation about the lightning and the church, and eventually the labourers went back to work.

Yet, for some reason, the bizarre notion that the Europeans still required the heads of natives for human sacrifice persisted; although it could never be proved, it was believed that Chinese gangs were responsible for starting these rumours. Like a plague, the rumours would surface every few years to disrupt the settled order of things, only this time, those involved were writing letters to *The Straits Times* to implore that the sacrifices be allowed to take place in order to appease the disgruntled spirits and to curry favour with the ruling *ang-moh,* the Hokkien phrase that translated literally as 'red hair'. However, the phrase was used as slang for all white men regardless of hair colour because it really meant 'fat, hairy, stinking, red-faced, drunken, long-nosed, monster-cocked, barbarian pig dog foreign invaders'.

Hawksworth tucked away his newspaper and sighed deeply. The investigation into the case of the dead American had gotten washed away with the rains. The American Consulate had sent him a terse note: 'Neptune defunct six months. No such man J. Caramel located Boston or Savannah.' It was clear that the Consulate's note was merely a verbatim reproduction of the cable they had received. No family or friends had come looking for the man or to claim his body: he was dropped into an unmarked grave in the *kuboran orang puteh*, the cemetery for white men at Bukit Timah, where he would lay amongst a jumble of sailors and convicts in the section reserved for unclaimed Caucasian corpses. The cost of the burial had been five dollars, borne by the colonial authorities; a plot and a headstone would have cost ten dollars, but because his name and nationality could not be confirmed definitely, and no one was willing to pay the fees, he had been buried in a pauper's grave, the naked corpse dressed in only a funeral shroud. Other than the coolie diggers and the cemetery overseer, no one else had witnessed the burial.

Hawksworth had other dead men to attend to. The wreckage of the ship was cleared. Any ice that may have been smuggled had long since melted away. Sitting before him on his desk that very morning was the paperwork that would officially close the investigation into the unknown *ang-moh* who had drowned in the muddy waters of Rochor Canal.

A knock came at his office door, and in came Hawksworth's immediate superior, Superintendent of Police Martin Fairer.

He was thick set, with a bulky neck striated red and white, leading into a wide coarse face and a conical head. Fairer's nose was uncommonly bulbous and crossed with purple veins that always seemed on the verge of popping. His mouth was thin, with lips the same colour as his skin so that it appeared like nothing more than a slit across his face. All told, the Superintendent looked like a projectile, although his eyes were kind and mellow, and his manner was generally casual among his own men.

'Good afternoon, David.' The superintendent was the only person in the whole colony who addressed Hawksworth by his first name.

Hawksworth rose and saluted, 'Good morning, Superintendent.'

Fairer half saluted then bade him sit. Hawksworth took his seat, while his boss leisurely took the seat opposite his own, fat fists on his knees and a book tucked under one armpit. Hawksworth remained stiffly 'at attention' in his chair.

'This just came in from London.' Fairer placed the book on the table. The gold lettering on the book's blue cover said *The Adventures of Sherlock Holmes*.

'A. Conan Doyle, sir?'

'He is apparently very popular. Have you read any of his books?'

'No, sir.'

'Mrs. Fairer likes to read these stories,' he said in a bemused tone. 'They are about a detective who solves peculiar crimes using only his unique mind.'

'Does not sound like my sort of thing, sir.'

'No, nor mine. The stories are far too fanciful for my taste, nothing at all like real police work. But since some of the other men have begun to refer to you as 'our Sherlock Holmes,' I thought you might want to become acquainted with the original,' Fairer said without the slightest trace of contempt or ridicule.

Hawksworth eyed the book with only mild curiosity. The comings and goings of a fictional detective were of little interest to him; what his fellow officers called him was of even less interest. Nonetheless, he nodded appreciatively to thank Fairer for the gesture.

'The book is not the only reason I stopped by today. It seems that we have received a cable from Madras. The India Office is sending over a man with regard to your investigation about the recently deceased American.'

'Sir?'

'He should be arriving within a week or so. Name is Welbore. No idea what the devil he wants – and I do hope we do not have to dig up that unfortunate man. Do we know where we laid him to rest?'

'Not the precise location, sir, no. But somewhere in the Bukit Timah cemetery.'

Fairer sighed and stroked his ruddy jowls pensively. The word 'nuisance' was softly expelled before he brightened again. 'Well then, back to my duties,' and he turned quietly to go. 'Enjoy your reading. No need to stand,' he said with a slight tone of bemusement.

'Yes, sir. Thank you, sir. And thank Mrs. Fairer on my behalf, sir.'

'She will want the book returned to her so do treat it with care. Goodbye.'

After Fairer left, Hawksworth opened the book. He idly read a page aloud:

But there was no great difficulty in the first stage of my adventure. Upper Swandam Lane is a vile alley lurking behind the high wharves which line the north side of the river to the east of London Bridge. Between a slop-shop and a gin-shop, approached by a steep flight of steps leading down to a black gap like the mouth of a cave, I found the den of which I was in search. Ordering my cab to wait, I passed down the steps, worn hollow in the centre by the ceaseless tread of drunken feet; and by the light of a flickering oil-lamp above the door I found the latch and made my way into a long, low room, thick and heavy with the brown opium smoke, and terraced with wooden berths, like the forecastle of an emigrant ship.

Through the gloom, one could dimly catch a glimpse of bodies lying in strange fantastic poses, bowed shoulders, bent knees, heads thrown back, and chins pointing upward, with here and there a dark, lacklustre eye turned upon the newcomer. Out of the black shadows there glimmered little red circles of light, now bright, now faint, as the burning poison waxed or waned in the bowls of the metal pipes. Most lay silent, but some muttered to themselves, and others talked together in a strange, low, monotonous voice, their conversation coming in gushes, and then suddenly tailing off into silence, each mumbling out his own thoughts and paying little heed to the words of his neighbour. At the farther end was a small brazier of burning charcoal, beside which on a three-legged wooden stool there sat a tall, thin old man, with his jaw resting upon his two fists, and his elbows upon his knees, staring into the fire.

'Is this what they think of as opium dens?' Hawksworth mused aloud as he closed the book. 'No wonder they think the East is mysterious.'

* * * *

A visit from an official from the India Office – who would have no administrative powers in the Crown Colony of Singapore – was decidedly odd. The fact that he was coming to discuss the dead American partly explained the oddity, but then everything related to that case was odd. Perhaps this visit would clear things up once and for all, although Hawksworth doubted such a positive outcome.

And the fact that Welbore from the India Office was coming from Madras was additionally wearying for the Chief Detective Inspector, for word about his youthful indiscretion may have reached the man's ears. The girl's sister had burst in on them on that hot afternoon in the back room of the icehouse by the sea, had then screamed, drawing a crowd from the adjoining tap room so that the couple were caught in flagrante delicto. Hawksworth still burned with shame at the thought. He remembered the girl's flushed, sticky face as she had kneeled before him, wiping her mouth with the back of her hand, eyes blazing up at him; he had stood there, his trousers pooled at his ankles, over his boots, his member now publicly limp.Out of his office, and walking into the evening air, Hawksworth noted that the gas-lit streets of Singapore seemed slightly less crowded than usual. There were not many rickshaw pullers running past the Central Police Station kicking up dust with their heels, nor were many workers walking back home – the latest head-cutting scare was already having its effect.

Hawksworth found himself on Coleman Bridge, gazing at the old Singapore icehouse, only a stone's throw away. It was as if he had been drawn unconsciously to it, like iron to magnet. The Malays called ice 'stone water,' he remembered, and he thought the name made sense in a practical way.

At the foot of Fort Canning Hill, across the street from the Assembly Rooms, was the two-storey wharf-side warehouse that

Grandfather Low had built thirty years ago. It squatted on a triangular strip of land formed at the base of Clarke Quay, between the river and the ornate grillwork of Coleman Bridge. Low had exchanged about sixty acres of a diseased nutmeg plantation for the land, which, because of the rise behind it, sat prominently, like a ship underway.

With its thick walls and wedge shape, the building resembled a bank, although frozen water was no longer kept under guard there. In a rare miscalculation of the market, Grandfather Low had overestimated the consumption of the product – the colonials used the stuff daily, but getting locals to add ice to their beverages had proven to be difficult, largely because the taste of pine imparted from the sawdust packing tended to linger in the drinks. Boustead and Company now owned the building and let the bottom half for storage while a portion of the upper offices, located in the prow of the wedge, had been turned into an unofficial clubhouse, where small time planters gathered for evening beer, punch, and billiards. Only the few old timers that drifted in for gossip had any inkling of the building's former purpose as a bank for ice: they would often speak about how the ice, after travelling for over four months and making two equatorial crossings had always stayed surprisingly solid, even during the slow rides in a bumboat from the harbour.

The Chief Detective Inspector, seeking coolness and perhaps even sociable company, found himself making his way towards the club.

The building was lit by gas lamps. Two long brightly patterned punkah fans were being pulled by thin Bengalis, who sat on cushions on the floor, half-hidden behind large potted palms, with one leg stuck in the air, toe tied to the pull rope. Their exertion was mostly for show, however, as the upper rooms, despite being beside the river, were inescapably stifling. Hawksworth broke a sweat as he walked up the dark stairwell. He could hear the sound of a small group of men talking from the brightly outlined doorway at the top. The men who frequented the bar were usually colonial hucksters, second and third sons of the minor gentry out to try their fortune in the plantations. Mixed in were one or two older men, the plantation owners, who perhaps had come to town to discuss business and were stopping off for a drink before heading home. But mostly, the bar's patrons were fresh-faced lads who had arrived straight from the backwaters of England to the far flung edges of the empire, to manage someone else's land. Most of them hoped to get home before they grew old. For them, the East was a temporary station, a place for them to earn their fortune. They did the best they could to recreate the bonhomie of home, but the most they achieved was a sense of martial camaraderie that left them perpetually uneasy, useless in the torpid solitude as they tossed with break-bone fever in the sweaty sheets under the mosquito netting of these distant lands.

Hawksworth surveyed the small cluster of young men arrayed at the long bar then ordered himself a stengah of whisky. One or two of the older men recognised and greeted him, and he moved into their circle of bodies and voices.

'Lost another coolie to a tiger this week. I suppose we will have to organise another shoot.'

'What is the bounty now?'

'One hundred dollars per pelt and head.'

'The natives believe that when a person is killed by a tiger, his *hantu* or spirit, becomes its slave,' Hawksworth said, to no one in particular. If he was not on a case, he was never quite sure what to say to people.

'Humbug.'

'The spirit acts something like a jackal, as it were, and leads the tiger to its prey,' Hawksworth then said.

'Ghost stories.'

'The dead man's spirit becomes so subservient to the tiger that he brings it to his wife and family, and then calmly watches as the beast devours them.'

All had fallen silent, quietly studying Hawksworth, wondering how a white man could speak of such rubbish, yet feeling some fear for what he had told them. This was not the sort of thing they liked to hear about, especially because they had to take long rides at night through the jungle to get home.

'Really, Chief Detective Inspector, do you need to talk like this?' asked one of the older men.

'Bloody right scary ghost story.'

'Imagine a ghost feeding his wife to a tiger?'

'Nonsense.'

'You were not here in 1864, were you, Chief Detective Inspector?' It was the eldest man in the room who spoke, a round balding man who had already imbibed too many *sukus*, or half-shots, of gin. Hawksworth recognised him as a gambier- and pineapple-plantation owner, who, in the larger order of things, was not a terribly wealthy man but was probably already worth far more than most of the younger men in the room would ever be. His name was Colin Lamb, and Hawksworth knew him to be a regular church-goer and a fixture on the weekend bridge circuit.

'No, Mr. Lamb, I was not here in 1864. I was still merely a lad.'

'That was the year we celebrated Her Majesty's birthday. It was a wonderful occasion. A little after five o'clock, there was a morning review on the Esplanade of all the troops and volunteers in Singapore. The sepoys mustered about eight hundred men – all of them wore red turbans and black trousers, and they looked very smart despite their sandals and hairy feet. Our artillery regiment numbered about one hundred and twenty, looking sharp in their blue trousers and jackets, and their white topees, lighting the way in the pre-dawn gloom. It was a fine sight, stirring.'

He had begun speaking to the room, his story grown somewhat threadbare from all the re-telling it had received over the years. 'We had any amount of fire from the assembled small arms, and twenty-one rounds from the guns of the fort. And then, in the evening, we had real magic. The streets were lit with gaslight for the first time. In point of fact, many of us had never seen gaslight before this, though of course we had read all about it in the London papers. A small illumination took place at the gas works, and then McMenamin the engineer threw his house open to all of us, and no end of champagne was drunk,' and here the man smiled a little at the memory.

'But one thing that greatly pleased me was to look down on the natives from the balcony. There were several thousand of them, or so it seemed. Several thousand upturned faces staring with wonder at the illumination. All that night, and in fact for several nights after that, each lamp post had a crowd around it, of enquiring Celestials and natives explaining it to each other. They kept trying to find the oil and the wick, and would touch the posts ever so gingerly with their fingertips, then pull back in wonder. They could not understand how fire came out at the top without the metal getting hot!' he guffawed. 'That is your native for you, Chief Detective Inspector. All superstition, and then stupefaction over any instance of modern science.'

'Too right! Silly bunch of buggers.'

'My cousin writes to me that in Cardiff people are always trying to talk to the dead. Séance, they call it.'

'I do not believe in such rubbish.'

'Hocus pocus.'

'You have never been home, have you, Chief Detective Inspector?' asked another, the middle-aged manager of some land near Jelita.

'By home, I presume you mean ...'

'He means old Blighty.'

'Great Britain?'

'England. You have never been to England?'

'No, I have not,' Hawksworth said, answering a question he was asked regularly. 'I was born and raised in Malaya.'

'Blimey! Imagine never seeing a daff?'

'Or a crocus!'

'Or a proper public house!'

'What else do you know about the native religions, Chief Detective Inspector?' It was the young man who had mentioned the séances, speaking softly with a pronounced Welsh accent. Hawksworth took a gulp of whisky. 'Have you ever heard of a *tuyul*?' He leaned in close, grasping the warm stengah glass and blowing hot breath onto the younger man. 'No? It is the spirit of a dead human foetus.'

'Disgusting,' said one, but the young Welshman listened attentively. 'Go on,' he said.

'This spirit of the dead unborn is controlled by a witch doctor, or *bomoh*.'

'Heathens.'

'I will not listen to this pagan idolatry one minute more. Come, let us play billiards.'

'Go on.'

'A person who owns a *tuyul* uses it mainly to steal things from other people, or to do mischief in their homes by sending it around at night while the owners are asleep. If money or jewellery keeps disappearing mysteriously from your house, a *tuyul* might be responsible.'

'A poltergeist! I heard about them in Hamburg, too. There is nothing Malay about Hamburg!' said a drunken man, laughing.

'Go on.'

'Once someone sets a *tuyul* on you, the only way to protect yourself is to place needles around your valuables. The spirits, for they belong to children, are afraid to prick their fingers, and they will keep away.'

'And if you see one?'

Hawksworth stayed silent for a moment, then said, 'One does not see them so much as hear them. They are tiny and they tend to scratch around the dark corners of the house.'

'He has given me goose skin!'

'How are these children-spirits controlled?'

'The *bomoh* keeps the foetus in a jar.'

'Disgusting!'

'With all due respect, take your native mumbo-jumbo back home with you, Chief Detective Inspector.'

Then, another young man leaned in, 'I know black magic is real. I was born in East Anglia. There are lots of witches there. Once, by the canal, I found a doll tied to a fence post upside down so it would drown when the tide came in. Gave me the willies, it did.'

'I heard about witches in East Anglia. Supposed to be bad country for that.'

'Catholic country is East Anglia, and always was.'

'The East is always primitive.'

'Can we play billiards now?'

'Go on, tell us more, Chief Detective Inspector,' said the Welshman.

He leaned back, the stengah empty now. 'I am about done, lads. It is a long ride home.'

'In the dark? Be careful of the spirits, Chief Detective Inspector!'

'You joke now, but you will not sleep too well when the lights are out tonight, Jack,' the one rebuked the other.

'Or when you walk through the bloody dark jungle by torchlight.'

'Enough for me. I should be getting home.'

'And you, Chief Detective Inspector? Does such talk of spooks keep you up at night?'

'And he lives in the blooming back of beyond, he does! Right in the thick of it!' burst out the middle-aged manager.

Hawksworth placed his empty glass on the bar top. 'Not me. I sleep like the prince himself.'

'Born and raised in the East, he said. What could scare him?'

'And never seen a daff in his life.'

But the Welshman and the man from East Anglia looked pale as Hawksworth made his way to the door. Walking close behind him, almost as if he were Hawksworth's shadow, was Lamb, the older plantation owner who had so vividly remembered the splendour of Her Majesty's birthday celebration. Once both men were outside, the older man softly called to Hawksworth. River Valley Road was strangely quiet; except for the one or two carriages that jangled up the street, the two men were alone.

He smiled sheepishly at Hawksworth, 'Good evening, Chief Detective Inspector.' The man was far drunker than he had seemed inside. He was turning fuchsia in the humid air, a patina of gin sweat on his forehead, which he wiped at with pudgy fingers.

'Had a bit too much tipple tonight, Mr. Lamb? Want me to help you to the hackney station?' There was one nearby, around the corner on Hill Street.

'No need, I can make it. I wanted to ask you about these rumours of a head-scare. I hear that the Chinese clans are clashing more than usual. It is a possible uprising?'

They had begun to walk along the river, which emitted a fetid odour – the tide was going out and was carrying with it all the waste and offal from upstream. They paused beneath a gaslight.

Lamb continued, 'My own coolies are mostly Malay, and they are beginning to behave strangely. At night they walk in groups to their kampongs. They tell me that something is afoot in the Chinese camps. In all my years here, I have not seen anything quite like it. Mind you, they are decent people, the Malays, decent hard-working people, except when they are lazy. Nothing as lazy as a lazy Malay, eh? Sods.'

'I should not worry too much about these rumblings and grumblings. You know the natives can get a head of steam up about the simplest things. It usually blows off.'

But the gin-sodden man was not listening, 'Mind you, they have stayed loyal to me all these years, know more about that land than any man ever will.'

'Where is your estate, Mr. Lamb?'

'Ulu Pandan. And no one is going to buy me out. I am not like the other planters who turn and run. This is my bloody piece of the East, and has been mine since I came out here as a young man with my good lady wife. That would be, I assume, about the time when you were born, Chief Detective Inspector. We are planting rubber now. Way of the future, it is, rubber. I am going to cover all of Ulu Pandan with rubber. Rubber will make all of us wealthy!' The man slurred his words, swaying dangerously as he spoke.

'Come, Mr. Lamb, let me help you to the hackney station.'

'No, no, I do not think I am in the mood to go back. I would rather stay at a hotel in town. Better.'

'In that case, allow me to help you to a hotel.'

Then, suddenly, Lamb began to sob, and reached out to

the Chief Detective Inspector to steady himself. Hawksworth at first thought that the man was going to vomit, but instead he was merely sobbing and blubbering. Hawksworth said nothing. Even the stoutest veteran planters were allowed to go to pieces in private from time to time.

When Lamb turned his face towards Hawksworth, he saw that the wrinkled features were contorted in terror and tears drained down his maroon face, shimmering in the unearthly green gaslight. He was trying to speak, but the words kept catching in his throat. Hawksworth grasped his shoulder, and the tears stopped. The older man mumbled apologies and dabbed at his face with an already soaked handkerchief.

'No need to apologise, man.'

Lamb blubbered, 'I have not been sleeping much, what with the strange behaviour of the workers, and the rumours of riot, and ...'

'Come on. Let us get you into a carriage and to a hotel.'

'And I have been dreaming.' He moved towards the dark waters of the river, 'Terrible dreams. Terrible, terrible dreams, Chief Detective Inspector. My wife ... I dream of my wife, my Caroline, she comes to me in our home. She comes and wants me to do terrible things,' and his eyes opened wide. He moved dangerously close to the edge of the steep stone embankment – one more step would plunge him into the filthy black water.

'She comes to me naked! Stark bloody naked with flaming eyes. Horrible burning eyes like red coals. And she chases me. She touches me. Wants me to feel her. Oh god, it is too much to even think about! And I cannot stop it, no matter how hard I try.

I cannot stop the dream as she makes me use devices on her body. In our home. In our marriage bed. She forces me to … Dear god!' Lamb paused then burst out as though deranged, 'Rape! She rapes me!' He lost his balance and tumbled backward.

Hawksworth lunged forward and grabbed the man's shirt just before he toppled over, then with great effort pulled the heavier man away from the edge. He fell backward himself, only narrowly avoiding the metal base of the gaslight, while the limp body of the older man fell next to him. He sat there panting, legs splayed out before him, breathing heavily in the thick night air, sweat soaking through his shirt. The inert upper torso of the planter from Ulu Pandan lay across his thighs.

The near accident had been witnessed by the Chinese boatman at the godown across the river– the main godown of Boustead and Company – and they were pointing at the two men, calling to one another. As Hawksworth lifted Lamb's head and looking into his unconscious face, he remembered something about the man: he had been a widower for more than two decades and had never remarried.

CHAPTER VIII

Welbore from the India Office

THE SMELL OF BURNT PAPER filled the streets of the Chinese quarter, wafting into Hawksworth's office as he finished the last of his *kopi-o kosong*. When the morning knock came at his door, he assumed it was Rizby and merely said 'come in' without looking up.

He could tell from the sound of the thumping strides that it was not Rizby, who walked with light agile steps, and he glanced up to see a short sun-burnt man standing before him, legs akimbo. 'Good morning, Chief Detective Inspector. My name is Welbore, and I come from the India Office.'

Welbore had turned up on the first day of the fifth solar term of the Chinese calendar, the fifteenth day from the spring equinox, the festival of *Qingming*, the Pure Brightness Festival or, more colloquially, Tomb Sweeping Day. The Chinese were bustling with filial obligations to honour their dead ancestors. That night, the *kongsi* would host feasts and burn joss sticks and paper resembling cash – 'hell money'. They would then offer suckling pig and steamed lotus buns, rice wine and whisky, to their ancestors back in the Middle Kingdom. During the day, visits would be made to the sunny hillside family tombs in Singapore, or, if required and feasible, to the towns in Malaya, to visit dead relatives there and offer prayer and paper and incense, and to kowtow before those who allowed one's own being to take form on this earth. More prosaically, in the morning, before setting out on the excursion, Chinese – poor or rich, in the dusty street before their shophouses or at memorial altars in their grand homes – would offer prayers to all those ancestors whose names had now been forgotten.

Hawksworth stood behind his desk to greet Welbore, but did not extend his hand. 'Good morning, Mr. Welbore. We have been expecting you. Please take a seat.'

'I prefer to stand, thank you,' the short man retorted. He was built like a pint-sized pugilist, with a thick torso and powerful arms, and thighs as big as saplings. His plush blond eyebrows matched a short-cropped head of hair, the burnt scalp shining red beneath. Hawksworth suddenly felt very limp and out of shape before the man; he crossed his arms behind his back, sucked in his small paunch and straightened his spine; however, he could do nothing about his thin, sparse hair.

'Please do sit down, Chief Detective Inspector,' Welbore told Hawksworth. The man had the palest eyes the Chief Detective Inspector had ever seen: they were the faint blue colour of very deep ice.

Once he was seated, Hawksworth could see why Welbore had preferred to remain standing: the two men were nearly on eye level now, with the standing official from the India Office only a few inches higher than the seated detective. From this angle,

Welbore looked impressively stout, as though a larger man were standing slightly further away in a perspective.

'First time in Singapore?'

'Yes, first time. Quite a show the Celestials are putting on this morning. I nearly choked on the smoke getting here.'

Hawksworth had seen plenty of these young men show up in the tropics before: they did not last very long. The little prick of the mosquito, and the bone rending fever that followed, was the death knell for most. The rest were bucked from horses or drowned in shallow waters, or they came down with fatal dysentery or were stuck with a knife in a brothel brawl, or they were sent home with a nasty case of social distemper or the Rangoon itch. Those on plantations ran into tigers or dissatisfied workers with razor sharp parangs, or they simply became infected with gangrene in a small wound. Most of these men lasted fewer than two monsoon seasons. If they made it to four monsoons – that is, two whole calendar years – then their chances of long term survival were greater.

Now standing before him was another sharp-eyed strapping youth, the picture of health. Hawksworth estimated that he would most likely be dead before the end of summer.

'I do hope you find our accommodations to your liking. I am sure you have already been introduced at the Colonial Office club?'

'Yes, yes, it is all rather ... Rather ...'

'Hot as the devil's arse and as wet as his mother's fanny – that is what the sailors like to say. We were told that your visit has something to do with the unfortunate American who was found in Rochor Canal?'

Welbore suddenly looked pale green and began to tremble. Hawksworth sprang up and around his desk to push a chair under the man while shouting out 'Detective Inspector Rizby!'

The fox-like face appeared immediately, 'Yes, sir?'

'Cold water for Mr. Welbore, please.'

'I am sorry,' Welbore moaned in his chair, mopping his brow, 'Not quite used to this heat yet.'

'The humidity is not very helpful either.'

'Thank you,' he said to Rizby, as he handed him a glass of water. After taking a few sips, he continued, 'Well, now I know why.'

'Why what?'

'Why you buried that dead American so quickly. In this heat, a body must turn putrid very fast,' and by the way he said it, Hawksworth knew that the man had never seen a dead man before, let alone one see one that had been left to rot in the tropical atmosphere, its skin swollen and black, baring a hideous grin where the lips had been eaten away, its eyeballs turned a viscous green, like rancid butter, dripping out of the sockets when the body was moved. Hawksworth had been there when they had pulled poor Lambert, the previous Chief Detective Inspector, out of the old tiger trap. Lambert had, they had surmised, fallen in accidentally, broken his arm and impaled his leg on the pointed stick, had then died a slow death, all alone in that dirt pit, broiled in that malevolent heat, tortured by insects. Then his corpse had been partially dismembered by carrion feeders before it had been discovered by a Malay lad, who had vomited at the sight of it.

And Lambert had been quite a handsome fellow, too.

None of this equatorial horror would do for Welbore from the India Office. The young visitor was an office lad through and through – a clerk, an errand boy, a tabulator.

'Indeed. We do try to get them underground as quickly as possible, in as Christian a manner as we can possibly arrange, of course. Here, do not drink too quickly, or you will take sick. Sip … Lean forward, as well … It will help with the nausea.'

Hawksworth returned to his seat to face the smaller man, who looked like a defeated boxer slumped in a corner of the ring. Rizby stood behind him.

'What is it about this dead American that is of such interest to the India Office?'

'Bit of a bother. I was sent here to identify the body. I have actually met him, the dead man. We played billiards together, one night in Madras. You have spent some time there, have you not?'

Hawksworth saw a flash of bright saris draped over lithe black bodies, of fragrant white jasmine flowers woven into long braids of black hair. 'I have been to Madras,' he said simply. 'Well, I am sorry to disappoint you. The office should have informed you that we do not keep bodies on hand very long here in Singapore.'

They had stuck Lambert in a box as soon as they had gotten him back to the road. The smell had been so overpowering that they kept him away from town and buried him at Bukit Timah in a quick ceremony the next day at dawn; the headstone was put in nearly a week later and had required a separate, more leisurely ceremony. Hawksworth had attended both.

'They wanted me to meet with you because you handled the

investigation. Otherwise I would have stayed in Madras. The weather is drier there. I find it more salubrious.'

Hawksworth thought again of Madras: He stood outside the thick white walls of St. Thomas Mount, where St. Thomas had been martyred at the turn of the second millennium, listening to the voices singing mass at the Portuguese chapel, the young men singing in Latin with Tamil voices.

'We do not know much about the dead American, I am afraid. In fact, we were about to close the case. We kept it open only because we received word of your coming here.'

Sitting up straighter, Welbore said, 'This American, if it is the same man, was in Madras not more than two months ago. He called himself Ned Bishop. He was a confidence man.'

'India had always attracted treasure hunters, mercenaries, all sorts of undesirables. Why so much interest in this particular American?'

'While this chap was in India, he managed to steal a family heirloom from the ruling Maharaja of Mysore, Chamarajendra Wadiyar. The tenth, if I am not mistaken.'

'An impressive feat.'

Welbore continued without acknowledging the detective's derisory tone. 'The India Office was hoping that perhaps we could find this man, assuming he was still in friendly territory, and bring him to justice in Madras. Most importantly, we would like to recover the heirloom and return it to the Maharaja. It would be of …' Welbore paused, searching for the apposite phrase, 'political advantage for us to do so.'

'And you believe that this body we found could be your man?'

'Yes. Well, I was hoping to ascertain that by seeing the body.'

'Do you want us to dig him up?'

'No! No, no need for that. Rather, might you have any idea about the whereabouts of this heirloom? In your report you have stated that the locals were generating rumours about a mysterious cargo that arrived with the man from Batavia.'

'That is true, but since the cargo was spirited away in the night, and since we had a body that no one was willing to claim, that was where we left the matter.'

'Nothing found on his person? Nothing in the hotel?'

'The body was nude when we found it, and his hotel room was largely devoid of any personal effects.' He thought better than to mention the Neptune Ice Company, still unsure as to why the India Office was involved in this investigation.

'You did not think to look any further into this?'

'One dead American? Some illicit cargo disappearing into the night? A ship burning? Singapore attracts as much riff-raff as India, but if the riff-raff can contain their problems within their sphere, then they are not our problem. They only become our problem when they leave their sphere, so to speak,' Hawksworth spat out testily.

Welbore's pale eyes flashed with anger, and Hawksworth realised that he had said too much, 'Which is precisely what this American did in Mysore. He left his sphere, and he mucked up very important relations with the Maharaja – that is why the India Office, rather than the local constabulary, is involved in this. And in turning up dead, he has become more of a problem to us then when he was alive. I cannot return with his bloody head on a platter, which is what the Maharaja, and frankly several highly placed people in Madras, want. Now I have to find this precious heirloom, which could be anywhere between Batavia and Mandalay, while you complain about the riff-raff.' Welbore collapsed back into his chair, flushed and sweaty.

'Rizby?'

'Yes, sir?'

'More water for Mr. Welbore, please.'

'Yes, sir.'

More calmly, Welbore continued. 'The India Office believes, given your background and prior involvement in the case, that you should be the one to recover the heirloom, assuming it is even still in Singapore.'

'How do you know that the American you are trying to nab and the dead white man who drowned in Rochor Canal are one and the same?'

'Without being able to witness the body, I cannot be certain of this. You have seen the corpse, however. Shall I describe him to you?'

It was the same man: Welbore's description matched that of the body Hawksworth had seen. 'As for the heirloom, with any luck, it is still here and can be recovered, ' Welbore sipped some water. 'Now, given my lack of knowledge about this country, and given that this heat seems to give me a perpetual fever,' he did not mention the horrible rashes and boils that were breaking out near his groin, 'I am going to sit it out for a few days while you look for the heirloom. The India Office would like to keep all this quiet, of course.'

'I must remind you that the India Office has no authority in Singapore. We are a Crown Colony and answer only to the Colonial Office.'

Welbore pulled a folded letter from his jacket pocket and handed it over. It was signed and stamped from the Colonial Office, the ultimate authority in the Crown Colony, granting Welbore extraordinary jurisdiction to oversee the capture of the fugitive and the return of the heirloom to its rightful owner. Hawksworth and his staff had been seconded to the India Office for the duration of the investigation. Maharaja Chamarajendra Wadiyar seemingly had some powerful friends.

Hawksworth whistled in appreciation, folding the letter flat on his desk. The young man attempted a weak smile. Now that he had delivered the letter, the important work would be left to the seasoned professionals.

'And the heirloom in question? Any description for me?'

'I have never seen it, but I do have this.' Welbore produced an envelope. In it was a short note, written in an ornate hand and illustrated with a charcoal drawing: 'Bronze statue. Apsara (temple dancer). Chola. Circa 1010–1050. Siva temple of Tanjore. Height 15.75 inches.'

The drawing depicted a young female, her long fingers posed in an exquisite *prithvi mudra,* the tips of her thumb and ring finger touching, as her body sinuously dipped to one side. A diaphanous blouse failed to conceal melon-shaped breasts, a narrow waist and a plump posterior. She wore a conical headdress, peaked like a pagoda. Her face was passive, adorned with a beatific smile that promised both sensual release and inner peace.

On the reverse, written in the same hand, was a scrap of verse: 'Then from the agitated deep up sprung the legion of Apsarases, so named that to the watery element they owed their being. Myriads were they born, and all in vesture heavenly clad, and heavenly gems: Yet more divine their native semblance, rich with all the gifts of grace, of youth and beauty. A train innumerous followed; yet thus fair, nor god nor demon sought their wedded love: Thus Raghava! They still retain their charms. The common treasure of the host of heaven.'

Hawksworth placed the envelope and its contents onto his desk. 'It is a bronze statue of a divine dancer, originating from a temple in Tanjore. However, for our immediate needs, it suffices for us to merely know that this as the stolen property of the Maharaja of Mysore,' he explained to Welbore.

'I was told that it was a bronze ... Apsara, I think was the word. Do you know what that means?'

'The barge she sat in, like a burnished throne, burnt on the water. The poop was beaten gold, purple the sails, and so perfumed that the winds were love-sick with them; the oars were silver, which to the tune of flutes kept stroke, and made the water which they beat to follow faster, as amorous of their strokes.'

Welbore stared at Hawksworth in consternation, 'Good lord, what is that?' he sputtered.

'Poetry, Mr. Welbore.'

The young India Office agent rose unsteadily. 'I will be at the Rochester Hotel.' He fell silent as he made for the door, his face now pale and damp. 'Damn this blasted heat!'

'Detective Inspector Rizby, please see to it that Mr. Welbore is safely escorted into a rickshaw. Oh, and if you want some advice, Welbore, stay away from European food in this climate. It is too heavy. Eat fruit and rice during the day, fish and mutton curries in the morning and at night. Drink tepid tea all day long. You will find yourself feeling better in no time at all, I assure you.'

Welbore glared in nauseated chagrin at Hawksworth, as though the detective were as mad as a March hare. 'Goodbye, Chief Detective Inspector. And good luck,' he spat, glaring at Hawksworth. Rizby gripped his arm and showed him out.

Once Rizby had returned, Hawksworth said, 'He will be down with fever for the next two weeks. Straight from London to India to the grave.'

'Too bad. He seems a nice lad.'

'They usually are.'

Rizby decided to change the subject. 'The poetry? Shakespeare, sir?'

'*Anthony and Cleopatra.*'

'Not with more glories, in the ethereal plain, the Sun first rises over the purpled main, than, issuing forth, the rival of his beams launched on the bosom of the silver Thames. Fair Nymphs, and well-dressed Youths around her shone. But every eye was fixed on her alone.'

'And what was that?'

'Alexander Pope, sir. *The Rape of the Lock.*'

'Well done, Detective Inspector, well done. I do not much care for the title, though.' Hawksworth thought for a moment, 'Poem about a card game, yes?'

'Yes, sir. And the snipping of the girl's hair.'

'What was the name of that skinny Kling that used to run crooked card games in Sailor Town?'

Rizby cocked his head and rubbed one earlobe. 'Do you mean Mohan Pillay?'

'Pillay, yes. Not the sharpest pencil in the box. I seem to recall he tried to double-cross a Chinese businessman, with the expected consequences,' Hawksworth said pensively, then spoke in a clear and definitive tone. 'Detective Inspector Rizby, we have been told that the Klings were there at the scene when the American's mysterious cargo was unloaded. We can now safely assume that the man's cargo is this missing statue. And we can now pursue the one line of inquiry we have not tried before: find out what the Klings know.'

'Do you think that Mohan Pillay will be of use?'

'He might be a huckster, but he keeps his ear to the street. If a rare statue was smuggled into Singapore under the cover of the night and then cost two men their lives, and if the Kling underground was involved in any of this, he will know.'

'He is still running card games in Sailor Town. I saw him there last week on Japan Street.'

'Good. Then tonight we will pay him a visit. Bring along two or three others. And Detective Inspector?'

'Yes, sir?'

'Bring your truncheon.'

* * *

'Boisterous tonight,' he heard Rizby say, though he could not see him.

Sailor Town was heaving with the additional population of immigrant Chinese who came to the old temples to offer their prayers to their ancestors back home. The worshippers caromed off the groups of sailors who were weaving through the dusty road in the violet darkness of late evening, some singing, others throwing elbows at the Chinese. Hawksworth towered over the crowd, shoving his way through; Rizby was all but invisible at his side, buried in the pedestrian jumble. To his right a fist-fight broke out between a coolie and a sailor. It quickly turned into a dog pile, the coolies overwhelming the sailors by sheer numbers, pummelling them down. Spread amidst this melee were hustlers and hucksters of all stripes.

The dice game that Mohan Pillay played from a stool in Sailor Town came to Singapore with Hokkien immigrants, but it quickly caught on with the other races. It was known simply as *lien poh*, 'turning treasure,' and required one die and a small metal box. The die had the same colours on all four sides, half red and half white. To play, a betting diagram was drawn on a square sheet of paper divided into four sectors. The person operating the game put the die into the box; the box was placed in the centre of the diagram then spun. When it stopped, the cover was lifted and the red side faced one of the four areas – punters who had bet on that area won.

To play this game with gullible drunken sailors required little skill but balls of brass. Mohan was as quick with a stick knife as he was with his voice, which he used to cajole unwitting seamen into the game of chance. That his die was loaded was a given.

That he was violent was a known fact.

As backup, Hawksworth and Rizby had brought along their four most loyal detectives – Sher Iqbal, Rajan Nair, Yahashan Vijayan and Mohamad Anaiz Bin Abdul Majid – to help throw a noose around Telok Ayer's Sailor Town. The two pairs would approach from different directions, while Hawksworth and Rizby would proceed in a circle. They each had whistles, hand and foot shackles and truncheons (he knew that Anaiz also carried a kris knife and, like Nair, a weighted sandbag; Yahashan kept a double-edged blade tucked against his ankle). When they found Pillay, they were to hold him and start blowing their whistles. The police wagon, with barred windows and a heavy lock door, waited for them at the bottom of Erksine Hill.

Pillay was to be apprehended by all means necessary, including extreme force if required. Two men would hold him; the rest would control the crowd while the wagon was brought around. At least that was the plan.

Voluminous smoke was billowing out of Thian Hock Keng Temple, the street before it jammed with Hokkien labourers. As they pushed through the eye-stinging haze, Hawksworth spotted Pillay's tall and wiry frame half way down the street, at the corner by the Nagore Durgha shrine – he was not alone. Anaiz and Yahashan were on either side of him: Anaiz was positioned behind him and was pulling his hand shackles out, ready to snap them shut over Pillay's wrists; Yahashan was about to grab Pillay's arms and pop them back.

Pillay spotted the Chief Detective Inspector at almost the same instant as the call to prayer sounded at the nearby Al Abrar

Mosque. Their eyes locked. Then Pillay shoved away Yahashan and bolted.

'Rizby!' Hawksworth shouted, but the smaller man had already burst out of the crowd of Hokkiens and was sprinting down the street. He had nearly caught up with Pillay at the corner of Japan Street when both men disappeared from sight.

Hawksworth moved swiftly on his long legs. Round the corner, he saw Yahashan sprawled on the ground, tripped by a bucket of smouldering ashes, surrounded by a group of berating Chinese. Ahead, weaving through the gaggle of sailors, he could see Pillay's head. He was already almost at Cecil Street, and beyond that street lay the darkness of the land reclamation mud flats.

Then he saw Pillay go down. Rizby must have caught him.

A dusky man stepped in his way and Hawksworth shoved him to the side, running at full speed now, pulling out his truncheon. At Cecil Street he saw Pillay struggling on the ground, lying face down, with Rizby's knees forced into his lower back, the butt end of his truncheon pressed against the base of his skull. Anaiz stood panting over them both, a pair of heavy hand shackles already open. As Hawksworth walked up, he snapped them into place painfully over the prostrate man's wrists. On the ground was Pillay's dice set. Hawksworth scooped it up as Rizby rolled the man over.

'Good evening, Mohan,' Hawksworth said with a smile, looking into Pillay's snarling dark face. The man was handsome, with high cheek bones and a full sensuous mouth.

'Oththathevadiyapaiya!' the man swore in Tamil. Rizby

smashed his truncheon against his head. Pillay spat blood, sputtering, '*Thaaioliongappanpundai.*'

'Hit him again,' Hawksworth said calmly.

Rizby swung harder this time; the man stopped swearing. Anaiz proceeded to shackle his arms. Yahashan ran up to them breathless, his trouser leg torn and bloody. A crowd was starting to gather around the men.

'Do not shackle his legs yet,' Hawksworth looked up at the mud flats stretched out before them, pitch black beyond the gaslights of Cecil Street. He could see the dim lanterns of floating ships flickering in the distance.

Nair and Iqbal showed up, pushing through the crowd. 'You two and Yahashan, hold these animals back. Anaiz, help this unfortunate fellow to his feet. Rizby walk him to Robinson Road.' Hawksworth pointed into the blackness before them.

The three detectives fanned out, arms held up and shouting 'stand back, you there, step away,' at the gathering crowd as Rizby propelled Pillay into the stinking darkness of the mud flats. At the empty corner of Robinson Road, just beyond the last reaches of the gaslights, they stopped.

'Mr. Pillay, I do not think my family would appreciate your description of them,' Hawksworth said, then rammed this truncheon into the pit of the man's stomach. Pillay dropped to his knees. Hawksworth kicked him until he rolled about in the filthy mud, coughing. 'You *pullusappi* cocksucker, get on your knees.' Rizby reached down and pulled the man up by his hair: Pillay bellowed in pain. Hawksworth glanced back at the rowdy rabble at the corner of Cecil Street, and at the three detectives who still stood there, their truncheons held out. An empty bottle suddenly flew from the depth of the mob, towards Hawksworth and his men, flying in a high arc, whistling as it turned end over end, and then landed with a soft thud only a few feet away. A riot was brewing: they needed to wrap this up quickly.

'Detective Anaiz, run round and get the wagon. Come straight down Cecil Street. If anyone gets in the way, run him down. Quick! Wait! Your sandbag, please.'

Anaiz placed the sandbag, a burlap sack sewn with iron balls, into his Chief's hand, and then ran for the carriage. Rizby still had not let go of Pillay's hair; he was holding the man up like a marionette.

'You see, Mohan, we could have done this nicely. I only had a few questions for you. But then you ran. That was your first mistake. Your second mistake was thinking that I do not know how to curse in Tamil. Now instead of being polite, I am going to beat you unconscious. Then I will chuck you into the Stews for a few days. Then I will come and ask the same questions that we could have settled over a cosy cup of tea. So this,' he swung the sandbag against the man's head, 'is a lesson in courtesy, you ignorant stinking pile of dog shit.'

By the fourth swing, Pillay had become unconscious, and they had no trouble – except for the empty bottles that were being launched with increasing frequency towards them – piling his limp body onto the back of the wagon. As it pulled away, one final bottle was hurled and shattered against its side, causing the drunken crowd to cackle merrily. They dispersed once the wagon had passed from view, melting away, returning to their temples and their brothels, to the toddy shacks and to the Australian girls at Original Madras Bob. None of them would be losing money to Mohan Pillay tonight.

CHAPTER IX

Geylang Interlude

CHAPTER IX

Geylang Interlude

OFF THE MAIN GEYLANG ROAD, which ran from town to the far eastern outpost of Changi village, on an unimproved and as yet unnamed dirt strip that ran deep into a vast coconut plantation, was the house where Hawksworth lived.

The house was an Anglo-Malay bungalow, the Malayan derivative of the airy single-storied box-like houses the British had built in India: In Singapore, they retained the wraparound veranda and the shuttered Western doorways and windows but added a high-sloped Malay roof (often tiled but sometimes covered in *attap*, the overlapped fronds of palms that the locals used for their own roofs) and raised the floor by several feet from the ground by means of brick piles. This local custom not only allowed air to circulate and cool the interiors of the house but also kept out insects, snakes, monitor lizards and other undesired guests; in flood-prone Malaya, this also helped keep the floors dry.

Hawksworth's bungalow was painted ochre, and it had a roof of glazed green tiles. Flanking its doorway were sealing-wax palm trees, what the Malays called *pinang raja*, with bright red trunks and dark green fronds. From the house's front veranda, the Chief Detective Inspector could peer across the unnamed dirt road into the serried grove of coconut palms, their trunks covered with rabbit's foot ferns and creeping lianas, stretching all the way to the sea.

On Sunday mornings, squads of amateur watercolourists from the suburbs would travel there to capture the ambience of the scene. They were mostly European or Eurasian, and they sat on stools, under the shade of big floppy sun hats and oversized parasols, before their portable easels. Even though they camped all morning long at the end of Hawksworth's lawn, apart from a friendly wave and a greeting, they minded their own business. Otherwise he would have chased them off.

The bungalow had been the home of John Michael Pereira, born in Malacca and once owner of the plantation that surrounded the house. He had the house built in the 1880s, when coconut had been a wise investment. He had then died of fever. The plantation grounds had been sold to the neighbouring plantation, and the house had remained boarded up for many years before Hawksworth had taken ownership of it.

Despite the house's seeming distance from the trappings of civilisation, the *attap*-thatched Geylang police station was less than a mile away from it, and Fort Tanjong Katong, with its two eight-inch Armstrong guns facing the sea at the root of the sweeping sandbar of Tanjong Rhu, was only slightly farther. Hawksworth knew the commanding officer at the fort, Major Peter Avery, who had previously been stationed in Penang, and the detective sometimes dined there with him, when he had time to talk about the hometown he had not seen in so many years.

Hawksworth had acquired the bungalow only when he had acquired a woman. Her name was Klannika Klinbubpa, but everyone addressed her simply as Ni (sounds like 'knee,' she would say). Before he had acquired it, fixed it up and then filled it up with furniture, he had roomed with the other single police near the old station house on Hill Street.

Ni had been working as a washerwoman in an unlicensed brothel – and perhaps as extra talent on a busy night – when Hawksworth had found her. She spoke little Chinese and almost no English, though she quickly picked up a fair amount of Malay. She was from Bangkok and had come down to Singapore to work as a domestic help in the house of a Chinese merchant who had developed a taste for the petite ladies who lived along the narrow canals the Siamese call *khlongs*. She had been mortified to learn that part of her duties was to allow the merchant, as well as his teenage son, access to her sex. She had fled their home, only to find shelter in a rough brothel that kept a roll of international women who specialised in servicing sailors.

Fortunately the brothel keeper was kind-hearted and allowed Ni to spend most of her time merely washing the soiled linen and not servicing the clientele. Unfortunately, the brothel keeper was also cheap and missed making one too many payoffs to the uniformed constables. Hawksworth, a Detective Inspector then and only fresh back from Madras, had led the raid.

Klannika Klinbubpa had clung to him during the ruckus like a snapping turtle, her delicate fingers, coarsened by her washing work, gripping his arm so tightly he could not pry her loose.

After the raid, he had installed her in a rooming house and paid her chaste nightly visits, to bring her food and small Siamese chapbooks printed on recycled packing paper, which he had found in a stationery shop in Sailor Town. They had talked to each other in their broken languages. She had tried to describe to him the life she had lived until then: the hyacinth choked canals of Bangkok; her voyage to Singapore on the steamship; the things the women did in the whorehouse.

After a week of conversation, he had bought the old tumbledown Pereira bungalow for a pittance, and the two had moved there. At first, she had cleaned and had done the laundry and the cooking. He had not asked for sex. She had offered that herself when she had decided, one day, that this was her house and this was the man with whom she wanted to stay. It was then that she came into his bedroom, unannounced, completely nude, and lay beside him, as she now did every evening.

Ni also did for him something that no other woman had – except for the rebellious young lady in Madras. Nearly every morning, in the pre-dawn dark, Ni would take Hawksworth's penis into her mouth and gently suckle on it until he had ejaculated.

The girl in Madras had been vulgar with the act, wiping the wet head of his member over her flushed face after he had shot in her mouth; it was precisely in this compromising position, she on her knees, lips and chin dripping, that they had been discovered. Ni did this lovingly, however, with a smile for him after.

She had a face only an Oriental, or a European raised among Oriental faces, would find striking. A wide forehead sat above bright eyes that sparkled with a quick wit. A straight nose rounded downward and flared outward at the nostrils, looking like a bell. She had succulent lips of a purplish hue that smoothed into a beaming smile. Her dark hair was thin with a slight kink to it, not like the thick silky hair of the Chinese. She wore it up in a loose bun most days, pulled back from her face. She was half his height; Hawksworth had to lean down to kiss the dusky skin of her broad forehead as soon as he came home, his large fingers nestled in her piled hair. When he had first brought her to Geylang, she had been a slip of a girl, barely nineteen years of age. However, keeping house and cooking meals and exchanging regular affection had put weight around her bottom and thighs. Now her breasts, with nipples coloured in the purple hue as her lips, swelled into a rounded bosom. Hawksworth loved her, and though they lived in sin, he otherwise treated her as man would a wife. He was aware of the rumour-mongering that his keeping the girl caused in polite society. But, as long as it remained behind his back, he paid the gossip no mind. It was not uncommon for a bachelor residing in the East for a long-term to take a local woman as a 'minor wife,' *pace* Coroner Cowpar and his Chinese amah. There were rules. Hawksworth did not bring the girl into town with him, and so long as he did not parade her about, her presence would not hurt his official position, nor would it bar him from the whist-playing parlours of the colonial elite. After all, no white woman wanted to touch him after what had happened in Madras. There had been some adjustments, between him and Ni, in the early days. He had insisted that she use cutlery and not her fingers when she ate at the table and that she clean her teeth nightly with the brush and powdery soap that came in flat cakes, called 'toothpowder'. The language difference was less of a barrier than he had expected, and over time she had learned enough English to converse with him, and he had picked up enough Siamese words to whisper softly into her ear.

She collected picture postcards, and at least once a month the Chief Detective Inspector would bring a new one home for her. Often they were of monuments and attractions in Singapore. However, sometimes, traders would offer him cards from around the world, and he was able to bring her pictures of ruined temples in Egypt or of great cataracts in Brazil, of bridges in America or of cathedrals in France. Her favourites were of Siam, which she would describe to Hawksworth excitedly in a mixture of English, Siamese and Malay, as she traced her fingers over the outlines of the image.

Of them all, she particularly treasured a postcard of the bronze statue of an elephant, black with white tusks, that was a gift to the people of Singapore from King Chulalongkorn to commemorate his first visit to the colony. The only time Hawksworth had broken his own rule and escorted her into town (under the cover of the quiet darkness of a Sunday evening) was to show her the Siamese inscription on the statue's pedestal and let her touch the thing itself: 'His Majesty Somdetch Paramindr Maha Chulalongkorn, the Supreme King of Siam, landed at Singapore, the first foreign land visited by a Siamese monarch, on the 16 March 1871.'

Pereira had left behind an herb garden beside the house, which Ni had restored, planting chillies, curry bushes, lemongrass and *pandan*. An umbrella-shaped papaya tree sprouted above the tidy rows, and a large jackfruit tree at the back of the garden, where the property ended and the coconut grove began. Directly behind the house was a *jambu merah*, a rose pear tree, the red thin-skinned bell-shaped fruit refreshing on a hot day. A woman from the market, whom Ni had befriended, had taught her to grow bright purple *buah naga*, dragon fruit, its snake-like green stalk wrapped around a wooden post with parts of old wagon wheels for crossbars. And there was also the night blooming jasmine plants that Pereira had cultivated and that filled the evening air with their sticky sweet aroma. At the edge of his property, by the road, was the old banyan tree, *Ficus bengalensis*, the strangler fig. Its base covered a third of the lawn, the over-spreading crown and adventitious air roots nearly another quarter of it so that the shaded part of the lawn was hanging as though it were an upside-down garden. The roots that stuck in the ground grew into thick trunks, and the tree had created the shaded grottos for which it was famous: this was where spirits were believed to lurk. Growing out over the road, the aerial roots were tied into knots, so those on horseback could pass beneath them unmolested.

The banyan in his garden had taken on special significance for the local people. It had grown over and around a stone bench, and as the tree grew outward, it had drawn the bench into its recesses, as if it were slowly digesting the stone. The way the strangler fig's roots had grown around it put Hawksworth in mind of pictures he had seen of a giant squid attacking a sperm whale, its tentacles reaching around the struggling cetacean and pulling at it, closer and closer. The bench appeared to be hand-carved from a single stone, and it certainly predated Pereira's house, as did the tree. What had been here there before this? None of the locals could say, although the villagers from the kampong less than a mile away considered the tree a *keramat*, a holy place.

On the roadside, not far from the stone bench, a small altar was built and used by the Malay villagers as well as the passing Chinese, their two spiritualities merging together. For the Malays, this was *datuk gong*, worship of 'grandfather,' the ancient spirit of the land, a mix of Islam and kampong animist tradition. For the Chinese, such worship was a form of *baishen*, paying respects to the *shen*, the spirit-deity that lived in the great folds of the tree, for the Chinese saw little gods in everything. A small tablet, once painted red with characters in gold but now weather-beaten and faded, was leaned against the tree, surrounded by several small joss stick urns and cups.

All shrines need a keeper, and as de facto ruler of the small estate, Ni took on the role of the caretaker of the little shrine. In the morning and evening, she cleaned away the ashes and burnt joss sticks and rotted foodstuffs left behind by others. Ni told Hawksworth that the phi that lived there was a nature spirit, a very old one. On the whole, the banyan shrine was beneficial for the Chief Detective Inspector, for by allowing the continued use of the place, he was seen as a good neighbour. He had been told that Pereira, a devout Roman Catholic, had sharply discouraged such heathen practices.

The interior of Pereira's bungalow was surprisingly cool. The kitchen and bathing areas were made of smooth brick; both Ni and Hawksworth used a wooden ladle and sluicing barrel, known as a 'Shanghai jar,' for bathing. A clapboard outhouse surrounded by baby coconut trees, strays from the plantation, was located far away enough that the odour would not waft through the windows.

The furniture in the bungalow was simple. There was a table and chairs, an armoire for Hawksworth's clothes and another for Ni's pretty printed sarongs, and a chest for storing the bed linen. The only decorations in the house were the silhouette portraits of Hawksworth's parents, facing each other in separate frames on the wall across from their bed, and the postcard of Chulalongkorn's elephant statue that Ni had pinned over her dresser. In the corner of the bedroom, which held only a horse hair mattress held on studs above the floor and draped in mosquito netting, was the long stock and barrel of Hawksworth's .577 Snider-Enfield rifle, the only weapon beside his truncheon the Chief Detective Inspector kept in the house. An old-fashioned armament, it was a gift from a departing police superintendent who had served in the British Indian Army. Hawksworth had not fired the rifle since it had been given it to him. He kept it oiled and ready for action, although he doubted he would ever need to use it. He was not worried about Ni touching it. Not only was it almost as tall as she was and too heavy for her to lift, but she considered the thing to be evil and wished he would keep it in the outhouse. The corner of their bedroom where the rifle rested was the only part of the house she refused to clean.

* * * *

It was a Sunday, and Ni had cooked an early meal of soupy lemongrass-seasoned chicken with vermicelli noodles in a clay pot on the charcoal brazier. They were now relaxing on the veranda, eating freshly picked jackfruit in the dimming light of the late evening, the sound of the crickets rising to an almost deafening pitch as the sky darkened. Ni was lighting a paraffin lamp when he spotted Gazali, the *bomoh*, the local kampong medical man, lingering in the gloom near the roadside shrine.

Pulling up his sarong, Hawksworth strode down the path to the road. On seeing Hawksworth, Gazali stepped towards him, a broad smile on his face, the palms of his hands pressed together over his heart.

'*Selamat malam*, tuan.'

'Good evening, Gazali. What brings you here at this time of day?'

'I am on my way to Kampong Serangga, to see a Bugis boy who is not well,' he said, referring to a mixed-race kampong that lay further inland, a little larger than the mostly Malay one where Gazali lived.

'I shall not detain you then.'

'I am glad to see you, tuan.'

'Tuan' literally meant 'lord' and was used as the address of 'sir' when addressing an *orang puteh*, a white man. Hawksworth certainly did not expect such treatment from his neighbours, but it would be impolite to correct them. 'I am always happy to see you too, Gazali,' he said simply.

The other man smiled but did not move on. Instead, a strange look came onto Gazali's handsome brown face, an expression of deep dismay. Looking Hawksworth in the eye, he said in heavily accented English: 'Something bad has happened in Singapore town.' His tone registered confusingly between a statement and a query, a tone that could not be translated into English, although the words could be. It was a tone that, despite Hawksworth's lifetime in the East, still occasionally caught him off-guard.

'Why do you say that? Did you hear of something?'

'No I heard nothing, but my sleep has been very disturbed.'

'Noises?'

'No, no,' and again came forth the wide smile as he struggled for the words in English, then simply slipped into Malay: '*mimpi ngeri.*'

'Bad dreams?'

'Yes. Dreams of a woman or a demon. I do not know which. Perhaps both.'

'I am sorry to hear that, Gazali. What do you intend to do?'

'Do? Nothing. I know the correct words to keep her away, so, Allah willing, the dreams will stop soon.'

'I wish you good luck in this. It sounds like a difficult problem.'

Gazali turned to go but then stopped again, and added, 'Strange, strange. Sometimes she speaks English, sometimes Malay, but when she ... *mencium*,' and he touched his lips to indicate a romantic kiss, 'then she speaks Kling.'

'Kling?'

'Yes, and then she appears very black. One black face, then many all the same, turning round and round in my head,' and he moved his hand around his head several times to demonstrate this.

'Sounds dreadful!'

He shrugged. '*Boleh tahan.*' We endure. 'Now I must make

haste. *Selamat malam*, tuan,' and he walked down the road to the edge of Hawksworth's property. But before he merged into the pitch darkness of the unlit road, he stopped one more time and, facing Hawksworth from that distance, raised his hands and eyes in supplication to the emerging stars and rapidly spoke something that sounded distinctly like either a blessing or an incantation.

Hawksworth peered after him, and then turned his gaze to the liquid radiance of the night sky, the Milky Way blazing nearly as brightly as the lamp beside which Ni sat, watching him from the veranda.

He turned back from the road and headed homeward across the lawn. Still thinking of the *bomoh*'s words, he uttered, 'By the pricking of my thumbs, something wicked this way comes.' He struggled to remember the next line; the words came to him as he approached his front door, 'Open locks, whoever knocks!' and they unaccountably gave him a little shiver.

That night, after Ni had gone to sleep, quietly, by the low dancing light of a coconut oil lamp, little more than a small flame guttering in a dish, he checked how much ammunition he had for the Snider-Enfield rifle and found three mouldy boxes stacked neatly beside it. In the light of the morning, he would check to see if the cartridges were still good.

CHAPTER X

Municipal Stews

As HAWKSWORTH AND RIZBY left the station that morning, they ran into Sergeant Major Hardie Walker marching swiftly out of the building, his khaki uniform rumpled and a disgruntled look on his face.

'Some trouble, Sergeant Major?'

'Aye. Nightmares,' he then muttered a few more words, but they were lost in the noise of the street traffic. 'Cannot sleep.' He rubbed his eyes. 'Thought a walk would do me good. Should learn to drink coffee, like you do.'

'We might have something to help invigorate you. We are on our way to interrogate a potential witness to the murder of a white man.'

Walker grinned, pulled off his topee and rubbed the sweat off his bald head. 'Aye, Chief Detective Inspector, that does sound a treat. Where? Outram?'

Hawksworth nodded. 'The Stews. Shall we share a carriage?'

A gang of convict labour was working on Outram Road, pouring crushed granite into the laterite dirt, tamping it down, so the carriage had to let them alight some distance from the prison entrance. While they walked across the shortly clipped grass, Hawksworth explained to Walker who the prisoner was and what they hoped to learn from him. Catching the man who had killed the American, Hawksworth explained, was of foremost importance to him. He wanted to know who the mastermind of the operation was: was it the dead American, or was he merely a stooge for some larger force?

At the outer gate of the prison stood an old Malay constable, Noorhakim Bin Mohamed Noor, Hakim for short. Hakim had been the gate-keeper at Outram Prison for many years, and they all greeted him cordially. In turn, he saluted the trio as he turned the heavy key and let them through the outer gate. Hakim's eyes were light blue from cataract, as blue as a Swede's, and his face seemed perpetually animated by a toothless smile. It was the last cheerful face the detectives would see once they had walked inside the prison.

The cells echoed with the voices of prisoners. Some must have been gambling for there were muted shouts of joy or anguish. From one cell came a melismatic voice, singing in a Johannesburg accent:

'The sleeping constables at night,
They snore like the rolling waves;
Patrolling streets for fourteen nights,
Will send them to their graves.'

The singer began again, the undulating melody turning into

a taunting chant, following the three policemen as they mounted the stairs to the interrogation rooms.

The Stews into which Mohan Pillay had been chucked were legendary among Singapore's criminal underclass. It was believed that those who died in the Stews were sure to wander the earth as restless spirits, forever looking for the police culprits who had broken their bodies in the prison dungeon. In the Stews, spider-like bogey men crept out of the stonework – for it was believed that a sinister complex of underground interrogation and torture rooms were built beneath Outram Prison – and flayed the prisoners, who were kept chained, naked and helpless, to a metal bed frame.

In reality, the Stews were two tiny windowless storerooms in the basement of the prison. They were comfortless places, where the masonry sweated rancid water and where inmates were forced to defecate in a corner, but there were no red-hot pincers or metal bed frames or shackles fixed to the walls. In a way, though, the reality was far worse than the legend: in the Stews, one had to sleep only feet away from one's own excrement, and in the Stews, one could see no light nor hear no sound. The bogey men would eventually emerge, but in one's mind, from which there was no escape.

Hawksworth let Pillay stew in this hole for the weekend, and then sent orders for him to be released. After Pillay had been allowed to wash up and eat proper food – steamed rice and vegetables– and was given a clean sarong, he was led to an interrogation room, where he was chained at the wrists and ankles to a chair screwed to the floor. A small table was set before him. He sat like this, blinking into the harsh sunlight of a high window, when Hawksworth, Rizby and Sergeant Major Walker walked into the room.

Hawksworth and Walker took up positions on either side of the table, as if waiting for their sullen, shirtless host to invite them to dine. Rizby leaned against the wall behind the seated figure, ready to speak for him.

Pillay's face was badly bruised from the beating he had received with the burlap sandbag. He observed them through one open bloodshot eye – his other eye was swollen shut – but he said nothing.

'Good afternoon, Mohan,' Hawksworth said, noting the damage he had wreaked on the man. 'Had a good rest in the Stews? Ready to answer our questions?'

The man nodded, resentment and hatred shining in his open eye. Walker unshackled his wrists but left his ankles bound to the chair.

Hawksworth took out Pillay's *lien poh* box and set it on the table. 'We are going to play a game. I will ask you a question. You will supply an answer. We will then shake your treasure box. If the top white side faces you, you are telling the truth. If the top red side faces you, you are lying.'

'And then I get to hit you, you black bastard,' Walker hissed. 'I would like to call this game "Silly Bugger".'

'As you wish, Sergeant Major,' Hawksworth said with a wink. 'Shall we begin?'

'Wait. I have a new piece of equipment I want to try.' Walker pulled from his pocket a piece of heavy and flat metal, made of dull brass and with four round slots: he slipped the fingers of his right hand into the slots, and then made a fist.

'Good lord man, what is that?' Hawksworth asked, genuinely taken aback. 'This comes from America. They call them brass knuckles,' Walker said brightly. He leaned forward and rubbed the blunt edge of the knuckleduster against the bruised pulp of Pillay's face. 'What was it again? I get to hit him if the red one comes up?'

Pillay jerked his head away in fear, pleading with his good eye. 'Stop, please! I will tell you everything you want to know,' Rizby translated Pillay's screams into English.

'Yes, I am sure you will. But what about the Sergeant Major's game? He still wants to play it.'

'Silly bugger,' Walker grinned.

'Are you not a gambling man, Mohan? What is the matter? You do not like the odds?'

'Please! I will give you what you want!'

'Hands flat on the table!' Walker barked. 'Enough wasting time.'

'About six weeks ago, an American was found drowned in Rochor Canal. What do you know about it?'

Pillay nodded, and then spoke, Rizby again translating his Tamil words. 'I know who found the *ang-moh*'s body and stripped his clothes and stole his watch and ring.'

Hawksworth shook the *poh* box and tossed the die on the table. Red. Walker lightly struck Pillay with his left hand, without the brass knuckles.

'Sorry, Mohan. Want to try again?'

'I do not know who killed him! I only know who stole his

belongings. He was already dead.'

The box was given another shake: the die turned up red again. This time Walker punched Pillay hard into his bony shoulder with the brass knuckles, causing him to shout out in pain. 'It is true! I do not know who killed him.'

'I do not think this die is loaded in your favour,' said Hawksworth, picking it up. 'The American came on a ship with a Kling crew. Who are they?'

Pillay looked askance, and then said, 'They are outsiders, from Madras.'

This time the die came up white. Walker snorted.

'Where are they?'

'They left Singapore the next day.'

The *poh* box shook: red. Walker rapped the knuckleduster hard against the back of the man's flattened hand. He screamed, tears rolling down his puffy face. Rizby frowned, shifting uncomfortably behind them.

'Stop! Please stop!' Pillay implored, 'I am telling you the truth! They came here from Madras and stayed for one night, in a house in Rochor, then left the next day. I do not know where they went.'

Hawksworth left the die on the table. 'Why were they here?'

'I do not know – they came with the *ang-moh* and brought along something expensive, some sort of treasure.'

'Did they kill the American? Who burnt the ship they arrived on?'

Pillay shrugged in pained exasperation, his cheeks moist, 'I do not know.' Walker rose and walked around him, placed one meaty hand on his right shoulder.

'Who hired them? What did they bring in? Tell me everything you know about them and tell me how you know,' Hawksworth demanded through Rizby. Walker started rubbing the metal face of the knuckles up and down the nape of Pillay's neck.

'A cousin of a friend was paid to bring them food. He heard that they were very afraid of the thing they had brought into Singapore. He had heard them talking among themselves, that they wanted to get it as far away from them as they could. Then, the next day, they were gone. That is all I know, I swear. Please, do not hit me again.'

Hawksworth glanced at Rizby, who nodded his assent. Pillay was telling the truth.

'One last question. Who owns the house where they stayed?'

'Chettiar. Subramanian Chettiar.'

Rizby nodded: Pillay was speaking the truth again.

Hawksworth picked up the *poh* box. He tossed it one last time: red.

'Not your lucky day, Mohan.'

Walker smashed his knuckled fist as hard as he could into the Mohan's right shoulder, tipping the chair and the restrained man onto the ground, where he lay crumpled, whimpering in pain. Hawksworth squatted down, close to Pillay's face. 'We will release you. Go home and rest. Recover for a few days. Then get yourself on a boat to anywhere, as far from Singapore as you can go. Because if I see you on the streets again, I will beat you so hard your shit will run out of your mouth.'

'Silly bugger,' Walker said as Hawksworth righted both the

fallen chair and the fallen man.

As he walked out, Rizby spoke to Pillay in Tamil, 'You better listen to him. For your own good, leave Singapore as soon as you can.'

As the three policemen walked out of the prison grounds, Hawksworth noticed that Walker was frowning. 'Are you alright, Sergeant Major? You look ill.'

'Bloody brass knuckles. Think I broke my pinkie,' he spat, and then audibly snapped the bone of his little finger back into place. 'Black bastard,' he muttered.

* * * *

The visit to the prison as well as the noonday heat had robbed Hawksworth of his appetite. Before he would visit Subramanian Chettiar to ask about the whereabouts of the statue, he first wanted to know why this object was so valuable – so valuable that men were prepared to kill for it. Hawksworth tucked into his pocket the description that Welbore had given him and directed a rickshaw to the Raffles Museum and Library, the stately domed building located near the old European cemetery at Fort Canning Hill. It had been an ambition of Stamford Raffles that educational institutions play a key role in his new model colony. After several permutations and relocations, the new palace of learning – what the Malay called *rumah kitab*, 'house of books' – had been completed in time for Queen Victoria's Golden Jubilee in 1887.

Hawksworth strode into the front drive only to find his way blocked by a dozen carts loaded with a heap of enormous bones.

The curator of the museum was on hand, directing the unloading of the carts and carefully cataloguing each bone, many of which dwarfed the men who handled them.

'Good afternoon, Mr. Towndrow. Got some new bones for the collection, I see.'

'Hello! Good afternoon to you, Chief Detective Inspector!' Towndrow put down his notebook, and the supervisor overseeing the unloading of the bones took this to mean that break time had started. He yelled out, and the coolies all but vanished in an instant. The two white men moved into the shade of the portico, where a skull about the size of a hackney carriage was sitting.

'What does this thing belong to, Mr. Towndrow? A giant?'

Towndrow laughed, 'Yes, but to a giant of the sea. It was found on the beach at Port Dickson, very badly decayed. The natives called it *gadjah laut.*'

' Sea elephant?' Hawksworth translated aloud, puzzled.

'Yes, amusing enough. I believe it is *Balaenoptera musculus* – a blue whale, most likely of the *brevicauda* sub-species, commonly found in the Indian Ocean. We are going to assemble the skeleton and suspend it in the main hall. Should make a popular attraction. But you did not come here to listen to me prattle about whales. How can I help you today, Chief Detective Inspector?'

'Your whale talk is fascinating, Towndrow, and I look forward to seeing the beast re-assembled. But, yes, today I am here for other reasons. I am looking for Theophilus.'

'He should be in the library by now. I saw him at tiffin, though I imagine he is finished. Go on through.'

Hawksworth thanked the curator then strolled through the

displays of stuffed birds and animals, of armoured insects and of moths the size of dinner plates pinned to soft wood, towards the library.

A small man, overdressed for the tropics, with thick spectacles magnifying his lime green eyes, sat behind the main desk of the library, propped on a stool, hunched over a book, chewing on a nub pencil as he read from it. A few wisps of unruly grey hair stuck up from his otherwise bald head. Theophilus Green, Chief Librarian at the Raffles Museum and Library, had forgotten more about Hindu art than most scholars would ever know about the subject.

'Good afternoon, Mr. Green.'

Looking up, while marking his place on the book with the nub, the scholar smiled when he saw Hawksworth. 'Ah, our good Chief Detective Inspector! Happy to see you. What brings you to this place of hallowed learning? Want another peek at the illustrated *Arabian Nights*?' he teased in a deep bass voice.

Hawksworth guffawed. Green was referring to an investigation into pornographic material in which he had assisted.

'Not today. Though the lady in question is indeed quite underdressed.'

He unfolded the description of the statue and placed it before Green, whose eyes widened in curiosity. He shoved his glasses up his wrinkled forehead, holding the paper close to his eyes, mumbling to himself.

'Yes, yes, the quoted text is from the *Ramayana*. I believe it is the Wilson translation, direct from the Sanskrit. Quite reliable.'

'We think that the statue described here was stolen then

smuggled into Singapore.'

Green looked up at him and stuck out his chin. Police matters were of little concern to him. 'What can I do to help?'

'What about this object? Do you have information you can give me about it?'

'Hmmmm ...' Green read the letter again. 'This is a Chola bronze statue. Chola refers to a Tamil dynasty that reigned from about 800 till the late 1200s, our early medieval period. A high point in their dynastic culture was a series of bronze statues, mostly of gods and goddess. They paraded them in public ceremonies.'

'Can you tell me if there is anything about this particular statue that would make it especially valuable to collectors?'

'If this picture is accurate, then the statue, though very beautiful, is typical of Chola bronze, nothing extraordinary. I am puzzled by this mention of it depicting an Apsara, however.'

'Apsara? Is that a dancing girl?'

'The Apsarases are semi-divine creatures – as it says here in the excerpt from the *Ramayana*. They are roughly analogous to our forest nymphs. Here, let me find a better description.' Green scooted off his stool and disappeared into the stacks behind him. After some minutes, he returned with a massive book: *Classical Dictionary of Hindu Mythology, Volume One*. His liver-spotted hands deftly flipped through the pages.

'Hmmm ... Yes, yes, here,' he pointed at a page, then read from it aloud, 'The Apsarases are the celebrated nymphs of Indra's heaven. It is said that when they came forth from the waters, neither the gods nor the Asuras would have them for wives, so they became common to all. They have the appellations of Suranganas, wives of the gods, and Sumadatmajas, daughters of pleasure,' he muttered, running his hand down the page. 'Their amours on earth have been numerous, and they are the rewards in Indra's paradise held out to heroes who fall in battle. In the Atharvaveda, they are not so amiable; they are supposed to produce madness, perhaps love's madness, and so there are charms and incantations for use against them.'

Green set down the book on the table. 'That is fascinating stuff! Do you see?' he cried, his bass voice lilting upward into a boyish enthusiasm.

'I fear, dear Theophilus, that I most emphatically do not.'

'Well, Chief Detective Inspector, there are depictions of Apsarases in temples all over India, and even in Java, Siam and Indochina for that matter. They are a standard part of Hindu architecture – somewhat like the angels in European art. What you have there is a very exquisite statue, but the subject is quite commonplace.'

'Perhaps the artisan who created this piece is what makes it valuable?'

Green shrugged, his glasses falling back into place onto the end of his nose. 'I am not an expert in Chola art. We do have one book on the subject, but it is written in Tamil. Perhaps one of your Kling officers can read it for you?'

'Do you know of anyone else in Singapore who might be able assist me?'

'There are several collectors of Indian art here; they might know something about Chola bronzes. There is one man. Chetty something.'

'Subramanian Chettiar?'

'Yes, yes, he is the one. He has been here once or twice, to seek my knowledge,' he chuckled. 'He then proceeded to lecture me on the very subject he had come to research. Typical behaviour of an autodidact.'

Hawksworth thanked Green then leaned over and grabbed back the description of the statue before it was snapped shut inside the massive book.

'It is a very funny coincidence that you are here today asking about Apsaras, Chief Detective Inspector. You see, I dreamt of one last night, and she delighted me in ways that even the illustrated *Arabian Nights* could not describe.'

* * * *

'So we now have a prime suspect but lack a motive for the crime,' Rizby said in exasperation.

Hawksworth was seated behind his office desk, describing his visit to the library. 'Correct. Chettiar was mentioned in direct connection with this case by Mohan Pillay,' he said, one finger held up. 'He has now been confirmed as a collector of the same type of statues that we believe the dead American smuggled into Singapore,' he continued, a second finger going up. 'Finally, I recall that when I met with Alastair Stewart at the Boustead Institute for Seamen, he said that he and Chettiar were in business to build a temple together,' he finished, a third finger going up.

'I do not understand the link with Boustead. Certainly he would not display a stolen statue in his own temple?'

Hawksworth pursed his lips pensively, still unable to see the entire picture. 'We shall talk to Chettiar tomorrow. I would also like to pay another visit to our friend Alastair Stewart to try and discover the exact nature of his business dealings with Chettiar.'

'May I ask what Mr. Green told you about the statue itself? Is it truly a Chola bronze of an Apsara?' Rizby asked with a note of consternation.

'Indeed it is. As I told you before, he said it was quite commonplace.'

'Yes sir, but he was certain it was an Apsara?'

'He was. In fact he pulled out a book and read out some chronic rot about these nymphs, which made them sound more like prostitutes than angels.'

Rizby swayed on his feet, a queer expression on his face, and he grasped the edge of the desk to steady himself.

'Feeling alright, Detective Inspector? You looked piqued. Sit down, I will fetch you some water.'

Rizby slouched slightly, leaning his hands on the desk. 'Yes, sir, I felt woozy for a moment. A peculiar dream kept me awake last night, and our conversation seemed to recall the ... sensation.'

Hawksworth cocked an eyebrow at the diminutive man. 'Go home and get some rest, Detective Inspector.' Teasingly, he added, 'Try not to let the bogey man give you a fright.'

Rizby smiled. 'There was no bogey man in my dream, sir. Only a Kling woman with flowing hair, woven with jasmine. She was very young, and naked. She parted her legs, then a lotus sprouted from her ... *yoni*.'

'Detective Inspector,' Hawksworth grimaced, 'is this

something I need to hear?'

'Before I could reach the flower, a buffalo demon emerged suddenly, out of nowhere, then devoured the lotus between her legs before he mounted—' And then Rizby was airborne.

The Chief Detective Inspector's chair flew upward at the same time. His head hit the wall and all was blank for an undeterminable number of seconds, before choking dust brought him back to his senses. He attempted to pull himself up, but slipped. He tried to shout for Rizby, but his voice did not work, for his mouth was clogged with debris. Spitting and coughing, he managed to clear his throat but then found that his voice still did not work. Neither did his hearing: the only sound he could hear in the room was a rushing, the sound of waves when a seashell is held to the ear.

Twisting up, he saw Rizby pressed immobile against the wall, like a mounted specimen. He tried to rush forward, then realised he could not – his foot hurt. He found it pinned under the heavy desk. He finally stood up, lifting the corner of the desk, and then hobbled toward Rizby, who was now beginning to move. A thin coating of dust coated everything, including Rizby, who looked white as a ghost.

Hawksworth took in a deep breath and recognised the noxious stench of cordite from discharged gunpowder mingled with the pungent smoke. The building was on fire. He yelled at Rizby but could not hear his own voice for the rushing in his ears. Reaching out, he pulled the smaller man towards himself, then hobbling, pushed at his office door. It was jammed. He slammed himself against it, and the door came off its hinges. The two men tumbled into a bedlam of white dust, grey smoke, hysterical men and burning cinders wafting in the air.

He dragged Rizby with him down the back steps, trying to reach the muster point located beside the stables. But once they arrived, he saw that chaos reigned there as well. No one was mustering. Suddenly Detective Sher Iqbal loomed up before him and got a grip around his shoulders. And now the three were dragging each other out the side gate, into the street, where already a crowd of gawkers was gathering. The fire brigade was nowhere to be seen, nor heard, for now his hearing was painfully coming back, as if a wasp were whining inside his ears. He shook his head. Iqbal propped Rizby against a fencepost, then ran back into the station. Smoke was now pouring in a steady stream from the windows on two sides of the building.

He walked around the front, and saw bodies and dismembered body parts scattered in the forecourt of the station. To his relief, the dead were clothed in uniform; none of them were his men. The fire was not as bad as it had seemed – mostly smouldering ash and smoke from burnt paper – but the explosion was worse than he had thought: it had punched a jagged hole through the thick front wall of the building, big enough to drive a horse and carriage through.

His hearing was now unbearably painful, his foot throbbed, and he squatted down under the blazing sun, his back to the smoking wall, feeling nauseous and weak.

The fog in his mind was beginning to clear. While he was being plucked up by unseen hands and carried out of the way of the incoming fire brigade, Hawksworth remembered something: in anticipation of larger and more frequent police patrols, they had begun to stockpile ammunition in the front courtyard of the Central Police Station for disbursement later that day. Something – or someone – must have detonated it.

CHAPTER XI

The Sport of Kings

IT WAS SHU EN, the pale-skinned gamine from the Mother-Flower house. He was sure of this even though he could not see her face from where she stood on the dais, covered in a loose silk robe. All around him was a discordant though not unpleasant tintinnabulation, as if thousands of glass shards were clinking invisibly in the air.

They were in a round building of red sand stone, with no windows or doors. The ceiling was open to the sky. Framed within the mouth of the circle, the cloudless blue was of an intensity the Chief Detective Inspector had only seen before in Madras. Hawksworth realised he was in a temple, the wall emblazoned with a bas relief frieze of curvaceous life-sized Apsarases, all of them frozen in a rhythm of unheard music. He looked up again and saw that Shu En was floating several feet above the dais now, her robe fallen away so that her small body was nude, her moonbeam flesh smooth and hairless. He could not see her face, nor could he call out to her, although her nakedness was causing in him an overpowering arousal; he looked down at himself and

185

he realised that he too was nude, with a painfully hard erection.

He tried moving toward the naked figure with the vehement intent of lust but found himself held back, rooted in place by unseen bonds. A panic set in, but it did nothing to diminish his arousal. The statues on the walls began to undulate and writhe, their sandstone fingers reaching out to grasp him, to reach his hard phallus. He tried to pull away, turned to see that Shu En's flawless skin was now crawling with ink, animated tattoos that mutated into strange maps and faces.

The clinking of the glasses grew louder, and he found himself on the dias, pinned beneath the floating figure, held in place by the strong stone hands of the black-eyed Apsarases. Shu En's slim pink vagina, coral pink like her lips, was above him, and beyond it laid the impossibly deep blue of the sky dome. The Apsarases began chanting in time to the clinking glass as Shu En lowered herself to his face, and he watched the slender labia pucker itself into a mouth, about to kiss him, and his own lips began to pucker, yearning to kiss its tender pink flesh, while tight fists of sandstone began to masturbate him painfully. He was close to his release, ready to kiss and lick the smiling line of her vagina, when a tongue of crimson snaked out from between the lips. He tried to clamp his jaws shut but found gritty fingers holding them open while the serpentine tongue moved in closer. He fought to move his head away, but he was held in place while the slimy tongue slithered toward him. When it slipped past his mouth, he came hard, a stream of red and white, of blood and semen, flowing out from his penis, and he could no longer breathe as the tongue blocked his throat. Hawksworth was suffocating, struggling for air yet still tingling with the intensity of ecstatic pleasure, when he found that he could suddenly scream.

He jerked awake, panting hard, unable to breathe in the hot stillness of the bedroom. He was covered in sweat and semen, which he found spread over his groin and thighs.

Beside him Ni was sleeping quietly, lips curled into a gentle smile, unaware of his nightmare.

He pushed back the mosquito curtain and swung his legs to the floor. The foot that had been caught under his desk after the explosion was incredibly painful, and he wondered if he had cracked one or two bones. When he tried to rise to wash himself, he found that his muscles were stiff, his joints sore, as though his body had been kept clenched and rigid for a long time.

The darkened rooms of the bungalow now seemed slightly ominous, as though the waking world had taken on a tinge of the uncanny, carried over from the intense dream. Sluicing himself down, wiping away the sticky mess, he trembled slightly. He had not thought of the pretty Hokkien girl in many weeks, and yet here she was in his dreams.

* * *

Ignoring the gaping hole in the front wall made by the explosion, Hawksworth ate breakfast, as per usual, at his desk at the Central Police Station. Bony white fish the size of his hand, their skins still on; runny curry with two eggs, fried; steamed rice; a plate of bananas: all of this was washed down with diluted but unsweetened lime juice, followed by two cups of black coffee served by Ah Fong, the office boy, a forty-five-year-old man from Hainan who had served in the police station since he had first arrived in Singapore as a lad of thirteen.

Finding information about Subramanian Chettiar would not prove difficult as the man liked to ensure that his exploits and antics, no matter how mundane, made it into the press. He was the youngest and only surviving son of a man who had made a fortune in Singapore, and he now spent his father's money freely, while casually driving his small empire into the ground.

The Nattukottai Chettiars, a mercantile caste originating from lands around southern Madras, to which Subramanian belonged, were prosperous money lenders and businessmen in their home district, and had been slowly building up a presence in Malaya since mid-century, not only lending money to fellow Indian merchants but eventually to European and Chinese businesses as well. Based on their prior experience with the British administration in their homeland, the Chettiars grew quickly adept at working the colonial system to their advantage – indeed a Chettiar managed the Imperial Bank of India. When Edward Boustead first became sole agent for the Hong Kong and Shanghai Bank in Singapore, Subramanian's father connived to make himself the de facto agent of the bank for the newly arrived immigrants from southern India. Boustead dealt primarily with other businesses and institutions at this own level; Chettiar, with his existing network of street-level money lenders, took over the more gritty operations. He eventually opened other enterprises, but it was this partnership with Boustead that would place his progeny in a class above their Indian peers.

The surviving son continued to live with his mother and wife and children in the bungalow on Serangoon Road that his father had built; but he had done nothing to continue to expand the empire. Instead, he had turned his attention to self-aggrandising projects, like the construction of a Hindu temple, which he and the current manager of Boustead and Company proposed to build near Dhoby Ghaut, at the end of Orchard Road. The temple was a brilliant stroke of social engineering: it would contribute greatly towards Boustead's well-known philanthropic ventures while elevating Subramanian to a higher shelf within the colonial social register, to a position far above his own people, the other second-generation Tamil families as well as the newly arrived migrants whose approval drove the man.

Hawksworth drained the last of his black coffee from his second cup of the day when Rizby entered his office.

'Good morning, Chief Detective Inspector.'

'Good morning, Rizby. Are you fully recovered from yesterday's shock?'

'Hearing is still a bit difficult, but otherwise I feel completely whole again.'

'No more nightmares?'

'No, sir, thank you for asking.'

'Had a bit of a rough night myself, although Ah Fong's coffee has put me right.' The tall man stood and fixed his well-worn topee on his head. 'Fancy a day at the races?'

'But the Spring Meeting does not happen until next month.'

'Indeed, Detective Inspector, that is true. However, there is a certain inflated money lender we need to meet there and ask about a dead nude American and a stolen statue.'

'You mean Subramanian Chettiar?'

'Of course,' said Hawksworth.

Chettiar's latest exploit was to get himself admitted to the Singapore Sporting Club as its first Kling member, and as the May races were coming up, he was at the racecourse at Farrer Park, watching his jockey running his only horse, a thoroughbred brought over from Australia at considerable expense.

'Given the importance the India Office had placed on this investigation – and given our total lack of progress thus far – and given what a bright and pleasant morning we have been blessed with today, we should spend some time at the racecourse with this man.'

'Splendid idea, sir. Should we bring along another detective?'

'Simply bring along your best Kling translation skills.'

On the ride in the hackney, he told Rizby about his dream, but left out the more carnal elements. The smaller man shuddered involuntarily.

'Sir, Apsarases are to be feared. They are capricious creatures and grant sexual favours easily, but generally do not like mortal men.'

'This piece of bronze is no more a threat to you than a Greek sculpture of Aphrodite. We are talking about a missing statue here, not a living thing,' Hawksworth said didactically, as though to hide doubt.

* * *

It was not difficult to spot Chettiar at the racecourse. He had pitched a camp for himself and his family on the open lawn, beside the regular viewing stands. The man was seated in the type of wooden deck chair found on steam ships, in the shade of an oversized yellow parasol that was held by a servant wearing only a sarong. Beside him, arranged on stools in the descending order of size, like a row of ducklings, were his mother, wife and four children, all of them looking miserable in the heat. Each of them held their own parasol, the yellow light washing their faces into a ghoulish shade of green. Judging by the nubile beauty of Chettiar's young daughter, the detectives could guess that his wife had once been just as pretty, yet the wife's beauty, due to the rigours of repeated childbirth was now greatly diminished. Sitting under the largest parasol was an old woman, the fat matriarch of the family, wrapped in a gold and green sari, a bright red bindi fixed onto the middle of her forehead. Behind the family stood the private carriage required to convey them back to their bungalow.

Hawksworth approached with Rizby at his side, trying not to limp too obviously on this bad foot. Sweat was pooling under his topee and streaming down the sides of the Chief Detective Inspector's face: there was no shade to be found on the racecourse, and even in the late morning the sun shone hot and bright. As they drew closer to the Chettiar camp, he noticed a little folding table with a platter of iced fruit – or at this point, fruit chunks floating in chilled water – placed only inches away from the patriarch's reach.

'Subramanian Chettiar?'

The seated figure unclasped his hands from his massive belly but did not turn to take look at the taller man. Instead, Chettiar wiggled pudgy fingers at the man holding his parasol, who leaned it slightly over so that half of its shade covered Rizby. Up close, Hawksworth could see that Chettiar's skin, purple toned with gold flecks indicative of Tamils, was smooth and fat. In fact, except for a few greys in his thinning hair, Chettiar looked much like an oversized infant, albeit one with elephantine ears with small black hairs sprouting out of them.

Clearing his throat, Hawksworth said in a loud, clear voice, 'I am Chief Detective Inspector Hawksworth. This is my adjutant, Detective Inspector Rizby. We would like to speak with you regarding an on-going police investigation.'

In response, without looking in their direction, Chettiar pointed to his horse and his jockey circling the field. 'Magnificent, are they not? Worth every penny it cost me to bring that horse up from Australia. The jockey I brought here from Madras – the only Kling you will see on the field come the Spring Meeting, and he rides in the name of Chettiar.'

Hawksworth moved swiftly forward to obstruct the view while Rizby moved beneath the parasol's shade, to stand himself between the man and his family. 'Mr. Chettiar, while I appreciate the art of horse racing as much as the next man, we are not here to view your new acquisition.'

Chettiar's face slipped from beatific calm to outrage. 'Chief Detective Inspector, am I under arrest?'

'Not as of the moment.'

'Then I would appreciate it if you would step aside and let me watch my—'

'Shut up.' Hawksworth stepped closer and leaned down,

confining the seated man to his deck chair. A drop of sweat formed on the end of Hawksworth's nose, and it hung there. 'I am investigating a series of very serious crimes, and all you can do is whine about your horse. What you will do is rise from that ridiculous little throne of yours, walk with me to the viewing stands, and speak with me in a civil tone. If not, I will arrest you here and now in front of your family and peers for obstructing the course of my duty. Rest assured, sir, that I would have no qualms, despite your exalted position, about chucking you into Outram Prison for many, many days.' The drop of sweat fell onto the back of Chettiar's dusky hand. The fat man did not move to wipe it away. He said nothing, but only looked indignantly at the man towering over him.

When Hawksworth stepped back, Chettiar rose. He stumbled out of the chair, one clumsy hand knocking over the platter of fruit with a clang. A few words of Tamil were spoken to his family, and then the two men marched across the uneven lawn towards the shade of the viewing stands. Hawksworth's foot radiated pain up his leg, but he kept upright and managed not to limp.

They stopped in the shade of the building, a travellers palm extending over them. Chettiar's face betrayed no fear, only barely constrained shock at the effrontery of the police. 'Now what is this about, Inspector? Do you know who I am? Do you know who I am in Singapore?' He pronounced the word as *sigha-pür*.

'Indeed I do, and when you decide to make your complaint, you had better make sure you get the names correct. To re-introduce myself, I am Chief Detective Inspector David Hawksworth, and that worthy man over there ensuring the continued safety of your family is Detective Inspector Dunu Rizby.'

Somewhat more calmly, the Chettiar said, 'Such a show of force had better be warranted, Chief Detective Inspector. You have me at your disposal, for now, so what is it that you would like to discuss with me?'

'Six weeks ago we recovered the body of an American man from Rochor Canal. He was nude and had been murdered. I believe that you are implicated in this murder.'

The look of indignation changed to one of dismay. 'What? On what grounds do you say such things? My family has been a respectable part of this community almost since the founding of—'

'Spare me your genealogy.' Hawksworth held up his hand. 'Also, I have reason to believe that you had him murdered in order to destroy evidence that you had hired him to smuggle stolen artwork from India.'

Fuming now, his face puffed up like an over-ripe aubergine, Chettiar sputtered, 'What nonsense! If you have evidence against me, then arrest me. If not, then I will have you prosecuted for defamation. You come here and interrupt my morning with these baseless accusations—'

'Shut up.' Hawksworth moved closer, almost touching the man's belly, which protruded like a barrel from under his white linen suit. 'I have yet to make an accusation – I am only stating my beliefs. Your art collecting is as well known as your family name.'

Chettiar continued in a less threatening tone, 'I need to prove nothing to you. One of the aims of my philanthropic efforts is to build a museum in my father's name that will allow the public, and especially the new arrivals from my motherland, to experience our country's rich heritage. If this noble effort is why you believe you have grounds to harass me—'

'I believe what I believe only with good reason,' Hawksworth barked. 'What I would like you to do, as a law-abiding member of our community, is to report to the Central Police Station tomorrow to answer questions related to this case. Your valuable knowledge of Indian art will certainly help us shed some light on this unfortunate affair, about which, and I have taken note of this, you neither claim knowledge nor admit culpability.'

Flattered and assuaged, the baby face smoothed into a smile, the head nodding vigorously. 'Yes, of course, I will be happy to assist you in your investigation, Chief Detective Inspector. What time should I arrive at the station?'

'Will nine in the morning be convenient?'

'Of course.'

The two men walked back through the blinding sunlight to the encampment of yellow parasols, Hawksworth's foot throbbing. Rizby was still standing behind the empty deck chair, where they had left him.

'Detective Inspector Rizby and I greatly look forward to seeing you again tomorrow morning, Mr. Chettiar.'

Squeezing himself into the chair, Chettiar said, 'The pleasure will be all mine. Good day, gentlemen.'

As the detectives turned to leave, Chettiar made sure to catch Rizby's eye: his fingers curved together to make the head of cobra, and then he snapped his fist forward, as if the cobra had struck. The detective jerked suddenly, as though he had been dunked in ice water. He remembered that he had seen such things before, as a boy in Ceylon.

'You will think me silly, Chief Detective Inspector,' he said in a low voice as they walked toward Race Course Road, 'but that man knows black magic.'

'Tosh,' the tall man said. 'The man is a charlatan and a thief, nothing more. Well, one thing more. He is our primary suspect.'

Rizby stayed respectfully silent but made a note to himself to stop by the shrine on Kinta Road on his way home. Considering the horrible nightmares, the exploding Central Police Station and the wizardly primary suspect, Rizby reasoned that he needed all the protection he could get.

* * *

The clean-up operation at the Central Station was proceeding with the swift efficiency that only a seemingly infinite amount of cheap labour could bring forth. Coolies had been brought in to clear away the rubble: even a large piece of masonry the size of a rickshaw had been hauled off. The litter of the interiors, the broken desks and chairs, the loose papers, had also been taken away. The soot had been swept, the blood mopped, the area cleared. The only remainders of the explosion were a gaping hole in the front of the building, the bent iron railing by the street and the lingering acrid stench of cordite and death that hung over the scene. Already the inevitable altar had been erected by the roadside, with joss sticks and candles burning before it, and with offerings of sweet bread and tea leaves left behind for the vermin to pick over.

Even Hawksworth's office door had been repaired, hanging on freshly oiled hinges. The Chief Detective Inspector drummed his fingers on his desk, his mind filled with Chettiar, the fat smiling baby face foremost in his thoughts. It was possible that someone possessed of such meritless high regard for himself would arrange to have the statue smuggled from India – and perhaps even would go so far as to have the smuggler murdered. But why ask an American to do the job? Why burn the entire ship? And what could possibly be so important about this statue? Hawksworth wondered all this, fingers drumming.

The coral smile of the moon-skinned girl flashed into his mind suddenly, desire pulling at him again. He yearned to see her, to wash away the horror of his nightmare with the coral lips and moonglow skin of the actual girl. Tonight, he decided, he would go to the Mother-Flower house. Perhaps she would be there. Perhaps they could smoke bhang together? Perhaps he could take her into one of the rooms below, strip off her silken robes, kneel before her trembling skin …

The reverie was interrupted by an importune knock on his door. 'Sir, I thought you might be interested to know that several of our men have also had disturbing dreams lately. I have informally inquired,' Rizby said, entering the room. 'The Apsara might be linked to this. They are known to bring forth such strange desires, like a succubus does.'

'I was afraid that you might find a spiritual connection between these things, Detective Inspector. But I think that for the time being we will stick to a rational course of action. The murders and arson and the stolen statue and our bad dreams are indeed linked. They are all indicative of the hurly-burly that we face daily in our rapidly growing colonial home. Progress is often painful.'

Rizby looked at Hawksworth, cocked his head to one side and rubbed his ear lobe. No matter how much time he spent among them, Detective Inspector Rizby still could not fully fathom the European mind.

Hawksworth was about to suggest that they have a bite to eat before sundown, but before he could get a word out, the door burst open and in rushed Detective Mohamad Anaiz Bin Abdul Majid, panting as he saluted. 'What is the matter, Detective?' Hawksworth asked quickly.

The sharp lips spoke without taking a breath, 'The *kapitan* of the Hai San has been found dead. Throat slit. Mutilated.'

'Good god!'

'When was the body found?'

'Only moments ago. Dumped in Macao Street.'

'Much as I feared,' Hawksworth spoke in exasperation. 'This means war has broken out among the *kongsi*.'

'Where is the body now?' Rizby asked.

'It has been taken to the death house, but there is no mistaking the man. Or the execution.'

'The Hai San would want the body back soon. Detective Inspector Rizby, you and Detective Anaiz view the body and make an official report to the Detective Branch. Send someone else to the scene where the body was discovered, so he can interview witnesses. Detective Inspector?'

'Yes sir?'

'You are in charge of this investigation. You are to gather evidence and nothing more. Make no arrests. Simply gather information as quickly as possible. And get there before the Coroner does and mucks up the scene with his apparatuses.'

'Yes, sir.'

'I am going to find Superintendent Fairer and recommend placing armed guards around the administration buildings and providing increased patrols in European neighbourhoods. In short, we are preparing for riot and war,' he continued in a lower voice, 'I do not want our zealous police force to shed any more blood than is going to be absolutely necessary, so I will find Sergeant Major Walker and talk some sense into the man before he starts sending out murder squads.' Everyone already suspected that the Chinese had planted the bomb at the Central Police Station: their nerves were on edge, and news of the *kapitan*'s death would only send them into a panic.

As they all rushed out, Hawksworth was shocked to discover that, despite the whirling plans and counter-plans forming in his mind, a singular regret had formed there as well. Under these conditions, he could not risk being seen going to the Mother-Flower house. His potential rendezvous with the pale-skinned Shu En would have to wait until this convulsion of savagery had passed. And beyond his own desire for the girl, he found himself genuinely worried for her. He had known Chinese gangs all his life, and was all-too-familiar with the grotesque violence of which they were capable.

CHAPTER XII

Tantric Night

BY THE NEXT MORNING, dead Chinese were turning up all over town. The corpses ranged from coolies to mid-level gangsters to one poor fellow who just seemed to be in the wrong place at the wrong time. Perversely, mutilations of the bodies became the calling cards of the clans: Teochew factions sliced off ears and noses and fingers; Hokkiens preferred cutting away lips and eyelids and toes; Cantonese bent limbs backwards, then took scalps. The mutilated corpses allowed the police to keep a grisly score card – it was the only way they could tell which gang was winning. To make matters worse, the plantation coolies had begun to align themselves with rival *kongsi*: the head-cutting scare had driven them straight into the arms of the waiting gangs, who offered them shelter and work in exchange for their loyalties.

The Chief Detective Inspector had stayed back at the station to deal with the impending crisis and was able to get home only past one in the morning; he left again for the station at five.

As he walked back into town, making his way through the morning mist that hung peacefully over the coconut plantation, he took a detour to Fort Tanjong Katong. Major Avery was having his breakfast when Hawksworth's arrival was announced to him. The Major wolfed down his eggs and curry rice, while Hawksworth, sipping on tepid tea, made his request to him. The Major agreed: if the fighting spread and the plantation coolies began to rampage – as had happened before in other parts of Malaya – the Major would send a detachment of troops to safely escort Ni back to the fort, where she could stay until the fighting ceased. Both men knew the brutality a gang of coolies would commit if they caught her alone in a white man's house.

When Hawksworth returned to his office, he saw Subramanian Chettiar seated there, waiting for him. He had all but forgotten that he had invited the man for a morning chat.

'Good morning, Chief Detective Inspector,' Chettiar chirped, a toothy smile on his dusky cherubic face.

'I am afraid that my morning is not very good – at least not yet. Thank you for agreeing to meet with me today.'

'Of course. I am always glad to assist the colonial authorities. We Indians can learn much from the British about being modern. In fact, just the other day—'

'Take a look at this,' Hawksworth cut him short. He placed the description of the statue that Welbore had given him on his desk. Chettiar leaned over to read it, but did not pick it up.

'A bronze statue of the Chola era? I own two such statues already: a Vishnu and a Lakshmi, which I purchased myself on a trip to Darasuram.'

'What can you tell me about the statue described here?'

Again Chettiar leaned forward to examine the picture, but

did not touch the page. 'This statue is exceedingly lovely, graceful even by the superior standards of Chola art.'

'Is there anyone in Singapore that you know of who would want to own it – other than yourself, of course?'

'Yes, many, many people! In fact, I think everyone in Singapore would like to own it. It is a very beautiful piece of art and a divine expression of spirituality.'

Sighing wearily, Hawksworth spoke quietly, 'Mr. Chettiar, may I remind you that this is a murder investigation?'

Chettiar's chubby hand smoothed over the wispy grey hairs on his head. 'Are you asking me if I know anyone who would kill another living creature so as to possess this ...' he gestured with melodramatic disdain at the piece of paper, 'thing? No, Chief Detective Inspector, I do not know anyone like that.'

'Where do you keep your art collection? At home?'

'My art collection? You mean my collection of artefacts of spiritual expression? Expression of a spirituality that is older than any other on this planet?'

'Our Chinese friends may disagree with you there.'

Chettiar guffawed. 'Chinese religion is playing with dolls. Recall that the Buddha himself was born in India and was steeped in our ancient beliefs. As for the disciples of the god of Abraham, I say that Christ and the Muslim prophet are mere puppies at the feet of Zoroaster! Yes, puppies! In fact—'

'Mr. Chettiar, I am asking you politely to tell me where you store your collection of ... artefacts of spiritual expression.'

'I store them in the safest place in Singapore– in the defunct icehouse on River Valley Road. It has the thickest walls in Malaya, they tell me.'

'You store your collection in the old icehouse?'

'Yes, the icehouse. You look pale, Chief Detective Inspector. Are you feeling alright?'

'I am, thank you,' Hawksworth mopped his damp brow. 'The icehouse is now owned by the Singapore Ice Company, a subsidiary of Boustead and Company. Is that correct?'

'The Boustead Company leases it to me to store my collection. As I told you yesterday, when you so rudely interrupted my family picnic, we are in discussions about opening a museum; it would exhibit art and artefacts belonging to Southern India and Ceylon.'

'I have also heard of your plans to build a temple with Boustead money at Dhoby Ghaut.'

'Indeed, that is true. The museum and temple are planned to be built within the same complex. I sometimes believe that the current director of Boustead and Company is truly Hindu, perhaps re-incarnated by some twist of fate into his Scots body.'

'You mean Alastair Stewart?'

'The same man. He understands that we live in *kaliyuga*, the age of degeneracy. He knows that during these dark days, righteous men must amass objects of light and share them with others who also wish to be righteous. Through our spiritual power, we can help to usher in the next age, the age of truth, the *satyayuga*, which will last for the next one hundred thousand years,' Chettiar beamed with pious expectation.

'I was rather under the impression that you were building these things as monuments to your own grandiosity,' Hawksworth remarked drily.

Chettiar bristled, and then straightened himself in his chair, his erect back pushing his belly outward, like the prow of a battleship. 'You are not one to speak to me about grandiosity, Chief Detective Inspector. Recall that I am here at your request. I could have hired a solicitor to come in my place, especially after the way you spoke to me yesterday, before my own family!'

'Enough!' Hawksworth rose to tower over the fat man. 'I can very well order you around, and that is exactly what I am going to do. Subramanian Chettiar, you are hereby remanded in the custody of the Straits Settlements Police under suspicion of murder. You are hereby ordered to surrender the keys to your icehouse storage facility, which will be searched. While this search is progressing, you will remain under guard here in my office at the Central Police Station, after which time you shall either be released or arraigned in the police court.'

Chettiar looked up at the angry man and smiled indulgently. 'I will do everything within my power to cooperate with you, and I look forward to my stay as your guest. As it happens, the keys to the icehouse are here with me now. Search the facility this afternoon, if you wish.

'I will do just that. Kindly place the keys on my desk.' He strode to the door and flung it open, 'Detective Inspector Rizby!' he bellowed. The fox-like man hurried into the room. 'Detective Anaiz is now assigned to keep Mr. Chettiar under constant guard in this room. He is to have no contact with any other person and is not to be left alone for even an instant – he must not be allowed to even go to the toilet. Yourself and Detectives Iqbal and Nair are to accompany me to the old icehouse immediately.'

'But, Chief Detective Inspector, Iqbal and Nair are currently assigned to the investigation of the Hai San killings.'

'Well, both of them have been re-assigned to this case then, for the duration of this affair. Proceed.'

Hawksworth shut the door and returned to his desk. The fat man was still smiling.

'Why are you smirking, Chettiar? Do you not understand the gravity of your situation?'

'You are enjoying your power, are you not? Ordering men around to do your bidding. Holding me here against my will. But it is only temporal power that you enjoy, fleeting and earthbound.'

'Shut your mouth, Chettiar, or I will shut it for you.'

'Where was all this power when you were in Madras? When you were caught defiling that young girl with your filthy discharge? You cannot keep secrets from me. Yes, I know all about you and your past, about the Jesuit orphanage and about the gross affair in India. Where was all this power then, Chief Detective Inspector?'

Hawksworth felt his temples throb, and his hands involuntarily formed fists. He leaped up, the room suddenly turning a deep crimson, the floor tilting as though he were aboard a ship. He towered over Chettiar, raising his fist to land a punch, when Rizby entered the room, Anaiz by his side. Hawksworth froze, and then lowered his arm. His foot throbbed painfully.

Chettiar laughed loudly, his eyes bulging in his childlike face. 'You will search the icehouse. And you shall realise that your luck will not favour you there, much like it did not at the icehouse in Madras.'

'Detective Anaiz,' Hawksworth rasped. 'Shackle this man's

wrists behind his back and to the chair's legs. Gag his mouth until I return. If he gets thirsty, pour water over his head. If he needs the toilet, let him soil himself. He can shit his trousers, if he wants to.'

'Yes, sir.'

The infant's face lapsed momentarily into fear, then smoothed again into a knowing smile. Hawksworth leaned close to the fat man's ear as the shackles were being snapped shut. 'I will see to it that you are executed before the next monsoon,' he hissed.

* * *

They had spent hours in the icehouse's dark rooms, their paraffin lamps help aloft to illuminate the faces of gods, of goddesses, of humans with cobra heads, of demons with necklaces of skulls, but they had not found the missing statue of the Apsara.

Hawksworth regretted that he had given Chettiar nearly twenty-four hours of time to hide the statue before bringing the icehouse's keys to the police station. He had been outfoxed. And he was feeling exhausted. He felt sure he was developing a fever. He sent Rizby back to the station with the other detectives and ordered that Chettiar be released. Of course the man would complain, and the Superintendent, in turn, would give Hawksworth a proper dressing down: for all practical purposes he had kidnapped a prominent member of the colony's business community for several hours. The matter would not go away silently.

What he needed, he decided, was a late afternoon drink. The Straits Club was conveniently close by on Hill Street. It was a poky, even gloomy, space: its potted palms, polished plank bar, worn out billiards table and neatly arranged parlour furniture gave it the impression of a sort of stage set or transfer room, a limbo where one waited to be transhipped to some destination unknown. Hawksworth was not a member there, but his position allowed him access, a privilege he occasionally used. The club's membership was composed mostly of upper-ranking civil servants, middling-level businessmen, planters and some military officers, and that evening, as Hawksworth slipped up to the club bar to order a stengah of whisky, he noticed a group of regulars seated nearby, talking loudly amongst themselves.

'Any excuse to riot, if you ask me.'

'Bosh! What the backward savages really would like is to control the opium trade themselves.'

'Too right!'

'They would bloody well like to get rid of us.'

'The Chinese could run the place.'

'What? You mean Singapore? They could not!'

'Chinese majority – Singers or Penang – could do.'

'But what about the Klings and the Malays?'

'Bloody lazy bunch of buggers.'

'It would never work. They all hate each other more than they hate us.'

'I think you will find that the Orientals respect hierarchal authority rather deeply. So long as someone sits on top of the whole show, the thing could work. They are not like the Irish.'

'I do not believe it. Maybe the Chinese can run the businesses but they cannot run a bloody country. I mean look at 'em!

Superstitious! As if they were living in the dark ages.'

'I do business with the Chinese, and I am always happy to. You have got to watch every penny with them, but when it comes to making money they know how to do it. It is part of their religion.'

'Tosh! They are backwards! Good at counting coins and mending shoes. Pulling my rickshaw. Cutting my carrots. Clipping my lawn. Sweeping my floor. However, they cannot run a bloody thing, the backward savages.'

'They can riot if they wish to, but if any Celestial tries to burst through my door in the dark of night he will get no better than the monkey he is. Deserves both barrels full in the face.'

'Hear, hear! Too true!'

The volume of their gossip increased as they consumed more alcohol. Next, they would talk about the strength of the army, then of roadblocks and seizures, then of mass roundups and firing squads – a martial fantasy that would carry over the next day, through the hangover, when they would look with gluey, hate-filled eyes at their servants and native colleagues. Hawksworth set his glass down quietly and turned to go, but one of the men noticed him, 'What, leaving already, Chief Detective Inspector? But you have just arrived.'

'Thank you, gentlemen, but I am tired and I need to make my way home.'

'Is there any truth in all this talk of Chinese riots? Are the clans really at war?'

'I hear the explosion at the police station was a Chinese bomb. They seem serious this time.'

'They are getting a bit big for their britches.'

'The clans are fighting no more or less than usual. The head-cutting scare is largely a distraction from the fact that one *kongsi* wants to control the opium farm. This will all blow over once the farm is assigned,' Hawksworth's voice quavered slightly. His speech did not even convince himself. The men nodded politely, and then went back to their drinking and talking.

'Excuse me chaps,' Hawksworth interrupted them, for he had suddenly remembered something, 'but do any of you know Colin Lamb, the planter from Ulu Pandan?'

A man with a smallpox-scarred face and thick eyebrows replied, 'Lamb? I have not seen or heard from him for a week. It is unusual. I assumed that, perhaps, he had finally sold out to Boustead and Company and was too ashamed to show his face.'

'Sold to Boustead? What do you mean?' Hawksworth asked with alacrity.

'I thought everyone knew – at least, all the planters know this. Boustead has been trying to buy his entire estate. Mr. Lamb always said he was too proud to sell, but I know that if I were offered what they were offering him, I would sell in an instant. Lucky man, Mr. Lamb.'

'You have not seen Lamb since when, exactly?' the detective was growing agitated.

The man thought about it. 'Since the other week, when he came to town. Why do you ask, Chief Detective Inspector? Is something amiss? Do you think his coolies rampaged?'

'I am not sure, but I know how I can find out.'

He checked at the station but Rizby was not there. Finding a rickshaw was next to impossible due to the head-cutting scare, so he did not reach the barracks near Sepoy Lines, where the unmarried policemen lodged, until nearly seven in the evening, half an hour before sundown. When he reached, he found that Rizby was just sitting down to have his evening meal.

He explained his hunch about Boustead and Lamb, and Rizby immediately pushed aside his plate (being sure to cover it in case he returned quickly and could still eat it), hurriedly grabbed his truncheon and revolver. The two of them set off for Ulu Pandan.

Rolling at full speed along Napier Road, the hackney carriage swiftly passed out of the developed sector, and into the plantations and market farmland around Tanglin. The compacted granite ended at Tyersall Road, and the carriage slowed considerably as it plunged forward on the laterite dirt. The darkness was closing in, the sky now turning a deep scarlet. Before they got to Ulu Pandan, they would pass through a large tract of undeveloped land.

Having grown up in Malaya, Hawksworth was largely immune to the romantic notions that European visitors attached to the jungle. The profuse vegetation, rolling endlessly to the horizon, was painted in all shades of vivid green, from the pea green of spring and the dark velvety green of endless summer to the yellow green of the plumage of the palm. The Europeans saw in this something fecund and erotic. What Hawksworth saw, however, was an inarticulate vehemence, a rapidly smothering fornication. The thick muck and the blooming greenery seemed to him a grotesque display of overwhelming indifference and misery. To Hawksworth, the jungle resembled a form of collective murder, a death orgy: the jungle fed on itself, and anything that wandered into it became part of this rank process of absorption and renewal.

It was near pitch black when the carriage finally rolled to a halt on the coral driveway of Lamb's hilltop plantation house. Hawksworth ordered the carriage driver to wait for them: the Malay shifted uncomfortably in his seat but agreed. He was given no choice: this was police business.

The whine of the insects was nearly paralysing, enveloping them in a cocoon of sound from which there was no escape. Hawksworth's foot was still throbbing, and he limped as they approached the two-storey house, a white Anglo-Malay bungalow, not unlike Hawksworth's own. There was only one lamp burning inside. Something was amiss, the men realised: it was suppertime, and the place should have been blazing with lights and activity.

The knock on the door produced a wizened Tamil man who did not invite them inside. He was quaking with fear. Hawksworth could sense, however, that it was not himself or Rizby that the man feared.

The man said little. He did not know where Mr. Lamb was; in fact, he did not seem to know who Mr. Lamb was.

'Ask him about Alastair Stewart.'

Again, nothing.

'And what about Subramanian Chettiar?'

At the mention of the name, the man grew more agitated. He bared a mouthful of black teeth, his gums stained bright red with the juice of betel leaves, and yelled at them to leave.

Hawksworth was about to push his way into the darkened house when, pulsing under the sound of insects, he suddenly discerned the rhythmic beats of hand drums.

'Detective Inspector?'

'I hear it, too, sir.'

'Now it is gone.'

'The wind has shifted.'

'Come!'

The old man shouted after them but did not leave the house. They heard him slam the door shut as they cautiously made their way in the darkness, ears cocked, hoping to catch the faint drumming.

Most of the land sloping downward from the house had been cleared for planting, and with a bright moon above them, the two men were able to make their way down a trail through the noisy night, the calls of insects echoing their footfalls. The drumbeats shifted with the wind, and after nearly an hour of wandering about in circles they finally found that the sounds were coming from over a ridge of uncut jungle vegetation, where there was light shining through the trees.

They pushed their way through the thick greenery, muck sticking to their boots, insects biting at their exposed skin, the sound of the drums growing louder as they drew nearer. Finally, they came to the edge of a clearing and saw dark bodies moving through a circle of bright torchlight. They realised that they had reached an old and disused Malay cemetery: the grave markers, round stone fence-posts set into the ground, were protruding pell-mell across the circle of light. The surrounding jungle had been left uncleared because Lamb had never planted this ground. This was a secret place, the men deduced, probably avoided by superstitious locals. Hawksworth and Rizby crouched beneath a fishtail palm – the Chief Detective Inspector realised with chagrin that one of the grave stones was beside him.

At the centre of the circle was the missing statue. She sat on a pedestal between two tall tombstones, garlanded with jasmine flowers and saffron ribbons. A rail-thin Tamil man, wearing only a loin cloth, was turned towards the statue, daubing her with something dark and sticky, dipping his hand into a copper bucket he held then rubbing the substance up and down her metal body. At her feet, lay a corpse wrapped in a winding sheet, fresh blood stains on its head and hands. Three more copper cups stood atop the still body. Hawksworth and Rizby, with a sick feeling, suddenly felt certain that the man was spreading human blood on the statue.

The drummers, three of them, seated to one side of the statue, now began to chant.

'*Tantra-mantra*,' Rizby whispered.

'What?'

'Black magic. They are calling forth a supernatural creature.'

'Bosh,' Hawksworth hissed.

'Should we intervene?'

Hawksworth counted about a two dozen silhouettes flickering through the shadows and smoky torchlight. 'No, there are too many. All we would do is scatter them. We simply observe now, and then pursue by daylight.'

The chanting grew louder, and the bodies began to move together. Then, moments later, the bodies began to move away, in pairs. Hawksworth realised with increasing horror that the bodies before him were nude, slick with sweat.

It seemed as though the entire ground was a sea of heaving bodies, vigorously humping against each other, rutting like animals in a cage. One couple lay down in the dirt, their heads and mouths on each other's genitals. An older woman knelt before a much younger man and took his penis into her mouth, sucked on it while he grasped her skull, bucking into it. Two teenagers were grappling with each other, rolling in the dirt like wrestlers, jerking and thrashing viciously.

Suddenly a nude white man seemed to materialise from the shadows, massaging his erect penis. He was holding onto a girl: grasping her under her thin buttocks, he lifted her and implanted her on his engorged member, then began to pump her up and down, while she wrapped her hands around his neck, black hair flowing. Hawksworth recognised them both. The man was Alastair Stewart. The girl was Subramanian Chettiar's daughter.

And then Hawksworth saw the infant-faced man himself. At first he thought that a sow lay before Chettiar, covered in the dirt, but then realised that it was an old woman, and she was on her knees before him, loose rolls of fat swaying beneath her. He was pumping into her from behind her, holding onto her hips. The man who had spent that very morning shackled and gagged in the Central Police Station was copulating in the burial ground with what appeared to be his own mother.

Hawksworth felt nauseous and looked away, up to the clear

night sky. The chanting was growing more intense, and now he could hear it perfectly, each syllable incising itself into his mind: '*Kama-kama-kala-ha-im, kama-kama-kala-ha-im, kama-kama-kala-ha-im.*'

The tall man found himself swaying with the chant, unbidden. His own penis grew erect, while a feeling of helplessness overcame him. He knew this chant: it was the same one he had heard in his nightmare.

Kama-kama-kala-ha-im, kama-kama-kala-ha-im, kama-kama-kala-ha-im.

The creepers in the trees above him began to writhe like snakes, moving in time with the chant, and the orgy unfolding before them began to move to the same rhythm. Hawksworth watched dumb-struck as the statue itself began to move back and forth on its platform, twisting, elongating, it's head a restless, turning flame.

He looked at Rizby, who was staring at him wide-eyed, his fingers in his ears, trying to block out the chant. 'We need to leave this place,' he mouthed. Hawksworth nodded, and they began to slide back through the jungle, away from the cemetery. Once they were away from the jungle and on open ground, they broke into a sprint, Hawksworth's injured foot reducing him to a hobbling run.

When they reached the hilltop house, the hackney carriage was still parked in the drive, with the driver sleeping peacefully. When they woke him, he screamed: he thought they were forest spirits come to deliver death.

Hawksworth did not sleep that night, for he was terrified of the horrors his dreams would bring him. He boiled water for the coffee grinds and stayed all night on the veranda, peering into the darkness all around, the Snider-Enfield loaded and cradled in his arms.

CHAPTER XIII

Evil Winds

IT STORMED FOR the next two days, the sky the colour of a rotten plum, lightning flashing yellow in low clouds, the thunderclaps loud enough to shake houses loose from their foundations. The wind bent palm trees sideways and uprooted hundred-year old trees while the rain lashed the earth, tearing away leaves and stripping paint.

Hawksworth rode out the storm in Geylang, suffering visions of the damned.

Gripped by a crippling fever, he could not leave his house for the next six days. Ni kept him under the sheets as the sweat poured from his body, racked with spasms of paralysing pain. She sponged him down with cold water. She boiled bitter broths that she made him drink steaming hot, 'to purge the evil spirit that had entered him,' she told him.

He hallucinated incessantly for the first two days. Often he was unsure if he was awake or dreaming, of where reality ended and the dreamscape began.

Sunspots on the wall became a kaleidoscope that spun about

in the form of a Flame of the Forest tree, the orange flowers shining bright against the dark green leaves. Shu En was perched in the upper branches, peering down at him with the head and face of a carrion bird, the pupils of her beady eyes blood-red. The slit of her pink vulva was visible, her *yoni* open to him. He was standing in the old Malay burying ground in hot sunlight, the sky spread wide above him, deep blue with an unreal intensity. A sound distracted him. It was cries of jackals, like those he had heard before in Madras. The cries then transmogrified into a chanting, and he recognised that it was he who was chanting: *Kama-kama-kala-ha-im, kama-kama-kala-ha-im, kama-kama-kala-ha-im.*

She flew down to him in an effortless arc, her head now human but faceless, with smooth hatchet-shaped flesh where her face should have been. Lines appeared on her pale skin, then the tattoos manifested, spreading like a stain across the chart of her parchment flesh. As they spread, the stains assumed the shapes of malicious faces that leered at Hawksworth, yet he kept chanting, watching her approach him. *Kama-kama-kala-ha-im, kama-kama-kala-ha-im, kama-kama-kala-ha-im.* The snake-tongue slipped out of the slim vagina and he knelt before it, chanting. She moved her narrow hips towards him and he opened his mouth in expectation of the kiss.

Ni was mopping his brow, her dusky face pensive and concerned, her forehead sweaty. She leaned over him, murmuring in Siamese and caressing his face. She had never before seen him this ill, and she was afraid. Her women friends from the kampong brought food for her – otherwise she would not have eaten, for she refused to leave his bedside for more than a moment.

After three days and three nights, the fever broke. By the fourth day of his confinement, he was strong enough to sit at the veranda. In the late morning, after tepid tea and a bowl of rice gruel, he watched Rizby make his way up to the bungalow. He had visited every day, although Hawksworth had remained unaware of his presence.

'Good morning, Detective Inspector.'

'Good morning, sir. Feeling better?'

'Yes, Rizby, thank you. Have a seat. Tea?'

While Ni fetched the tea, Rizby launched into his report. There was no good news.

He had returned with a team of detectives to Lamb's estate the next day, and through the storm, with great difficulty, had found the burying ground. But it had been empty. There had been no traces in the cemetery of the previous night's lurid depravity – the tempest had turned the ground into foamy mud. The plantation house had been deserted as well, the front door left open as if to allow thieves and animals to wander in. They had searched it but found nothing. Night surveillance had also proved fruitless. The Tantric rites had not been repeated – at least not at that same location. And Lamb himself was still missing

Both Chettiar and Stewart appeared in public, and seemed as nonchalant as they had always been. In fact, oddly, Chettiar had made no official complaint about having been held at the station and having been shackled to a chair. Rizby had arranged to have them shadowed, but he was short of manpower: the Chinese were continuing with their slaughter of each other, and every morning brought fresh corpses. There were not enough men to assign for the tailing of the two culprits; most of them were busy investigating and documenting every dead Chinese that turned up on roads and in ditches, as if sprouting out of the ground like weeds. However, based on the manner of the gruesome mutilations made on the bodies, they had been able to judge that the Hai San and the Low factions were winning the body count war.

One body, however, Rizby did bring to Hawksworth's attention. Mohan Pillay had been found dumped on Napier Road near the Botanic Gardens. He had been tortured, then beheaded. The body had been found the day after the two detectives had witnessed the strange orgy. Was Pillay perhaps the corpse under the winding sheet, Rizby wondered aloud.

'We need to proceed with caution. They know that we were at the plantation house – the old man would have reported us – but they do not know that we saw them at their ... ceremony. The statue will be well-hidden, and unfortunately, what we witnessed, though disgusting, does not give us enough grounds for arrest.'

'So we let them continue to move freely?'

'The clan fighting is more important: keep your men on that. If the Chettiars – and Mr. Stewart – want to screw themselves silly in the jungle at night, I do not care. Our goal is the recovery of the statue and the investigation into what now appears to be multiple homicides. Stewart is the weaker of the two. Once I am well again, we will pay him a visit. In the meantime, let them believe that they are in the clear for a few more days.'

'I understand, sir.'

Rizby returned at the same time the next day, this time with a bouquet of flowers for Ni and a bottle of arrack for Hawksworth.

'If the fever has broken, drink two or three glasses of this before you sleep at night. It will help speed your recovery.'

'Thank you, Detective Inspector. And what news do you have for me today?'

The Chinese bodies were continuing to pile up. Chettiar and Stewart were behaving normally. Now it was the European community causing trouble. They were getting nervous, and their requests for summoning troops from Penang were growing louder. But the war between the *kongsi* seemed to have reached Georgetown, and Penang could not spare its troops. To placate the Singapore residents, the Governor had ordered the eight-inch guns at Fort Canning hill to be swivelled away from the sea, toward which they normally were pointed, and to cover the Chinese quarter. The snouts of the weapons could be seen poking over the walls of the fort from High Street, aiming towards the civilian population.

'Good lord! Are things that serious? Or is this all for show?'

Rizby said quietly, 'Apparently, several of the prominent Peranakan families have shuttered up their houses and left for the hinterland.'

Hawksworth fell into a meditative silence. If the Peranakan families are decamping, then the situation was indeed serious. They were the earliest generations of Chinese immigrants to Malaya. They had been here long enough to partly assimilate local cultures – not only Malay but elements of Indian and even colonial Portuguese cultures. As such, they maintained cordial relations with all the races while keeping to their own. They were a good barometer of what the newer immigrant populations were tending to in their enclaves.

He turned to speak to Rizby, to ask about which families had left, but his mind was now wandering over the rice fields in the Yangtze Delta, following sailing junks up the Grand Canal, past palaces emblazoned with jade dragons, and past thousands of troops in shining armoured breastplates standing at attention atop the walls.

Hawksworth's head lolled to one side, hands left loose in the lap of his sarong. Rizby cocked his head, rubbing his earlobe as he considered the sleeping man. He left after saying goodbye to Ni, who came to sit beside Hawksworth and fan away the flies that tried to land on him.

* * *

Hawksworth awoke with a start when he heard voices. Yong Seng was standing on the veranda before him. Cheang Sam Teo, the orang-utan door guard from the *kongsi* house, was by his side.

Yong Seng greeted Ni in Siamese, much to her delight. After the two had exchanged pleasantries, she slipped into the bungalow, and Yong Seng sat in her chair beside Hawksworth.

'What brings you out to the countryside today, Tan Yong Seng?'

'We heard that you were ill.'

'Yes, a fever. Nearly recovered.'

Yong Seng nodded, '*Angin jehat,* always bad for health.' He meant the storm. There was a local belief that these sudden tempests from the south blew 'evil winds' from Java that carried fever and pestilence.

'What is it that I can do for you? Had enough of your wars and killings?'

'The *kapitan* of the Mother-Flower *kongsi* is dead. Yong Chern is now *samseng ong*, not only of the Mother-Flowers but of all the Hokkien clans. They have joined with us.'

'Yong Chern is now the big boss?'

'Yes.'

'And what about Shu En?'

Yong Seng smiled then laughed the soft Chinese laugh that meant affectionate surprise. 'You are so ill, and still you think of her? Wah! I did not know you were a man of such strong passion!'

Hawksworth made no reply.

'Here, I have brought you something for your recovery,' he held a bag. 'Ask Ni to boil these, then drink that water. Do not eat them.' Rattling inside were roots and berries and dried honey bees.

'Thank you, Yong Seng. Your kindness touches my heart.'

They remained silent for a moment, surveying the scene while the orang-utan man squatted and picked at his giant toes. The sky was still overcast, and the palm plantation was still damp from the drenching it had received over the previous days, the ground soaked, smelling of rot.

The Chief Detective Inspector spoke first. 'When will you bring this war to an end? If it spreads much further than it has, or if the coolies on the plantations begin to rampage, the army will get involved and much blood will be shed.'

'We have been told that they are now pointing the guns of

Fort Canning at the Chinese quarter.'

'I have been told much the same,' and Hawksworth had a momentary vision of the chaos that would occur if they actually rained down destruction on their own city: the people running pell-mell as the shells whistled overhead; explosions tearing away the facades from the shophouses; the bodies split and broken and tossed like rag dolls; dismembered horses laying in the street; the bare feet of panicked children cut to ribbons by shards of razor sharp glass; the screams of the mutilated and dying. 'You need to end this clan war swiftly.'

'Now that all the Hokkien clans are on our side, we will certainly win.'

'At what cost?' Hawksworth asked, although he knew the answer. The killing would stop only when the big bosses all agreed on how to divvy up the vice trades, both licit and illicit. At the very least, this war had pushed the Hokkien clans into a class with the Teochews and Cantonese. They would no longer be the scorned underclass of Singapore's Chinese gangs. By this war's end, they would be able to claim their own ground – assuming there was any ground left to claim.

'Yong Seng, I need to ask your help.'

'Of course, anything.'

'I am short of men and I need someone to watch Subramanian Chettiar. Can you spare a man to shadow him?'

'The fat rich Kling? Why?'

Hawksworth told him the whole story, from beginning to end.

'I will do this, not only to help you, my *ang-moh* brother, but because Koestono, the ship's captain, was my friend. If the Klings burnt him because of this statue, then our fights are now joined,' he said with murderous zeal.

'Do not kill him! Wait for me to recover the statue. We would also like to bring the man to justice.'

'I will give him justice.'

'Her Majesty's justice. I believe he also killed one of ours, the unfortunate Mr. Lamb. Rest assured that Straits Settlements justice will be swift.'

'As a mark of our friendship then, I will watch him and then report to you about what I find out. What about the Boustead man?'

Hawksworth rubbed his palms together. 'In a day or two, when my strength has returned, I will deal with Mr. Stewart myself.'

As they parted, Yong Seng said, 'When I see her, I will tell Shu En of your concern. I believe she is fond of you, too. She speaks of you often. It makes Yong Chern very jealous!' Then he laughed the chromatic Chinese laugh that meant humour at the absurdity of the human condition.

Hawksworth pursed his lips, annoyed at the man's levity in the midst of such carnage. 'Thank you, Yong Seng.'

'Get well soon, Chief Detective Inspector. I will remember you in my prayers.'

* * *

On the seventh day, the Chief Detective Inspector rode into

town, to the Central Police Station. As he passed the Padang, he saw army troops drilling under the hot sun, marching in tight geometric formations. This was another way to send a message to the Chinese. A Sikh patrol was now stationed on South Bridge Road, shuttling between the station and the Police Court building, guarding the main portal into the Chinese quarter. By the looks on their fearsome faces, they were eager for a fight.

Several men welcomed him back, though the atmosphere was generally glum. It seemed that everyone had accepted the fact that the clan war would soon peak and that the coolies would most likely begin to riot. European blood would be shed, then the army and police would swoop in with the brute force required to restore the status quo, regardless of how much blood they would have to spill in the process. What rioters tend to forget is that when push comes to shove, it is the authorities who will swing the hardest. They had the law – and impunity – on their side.

Once in his office, Hawksworth slumped into his chair and waited for Rizby. The tall man was still weak from the fever, gasping for breath. His foot had healed somewhat, but he felt grossly diminished. He had regained his composure when Rizby entered.

'Good morning, Detective Inspector.'

'Good morning to you, sir. It is a pleasure to see you back on your feet.'

'Thanks to the good will and kindness of my friends, the recovery was a speedy one,' he smiled at Rizby.

'What is on the agenda for today, sir?'

'Get your shackles. Today we are going to bring in Mr.

Stewart for questioning.'

'When, sir?'

'Right now.'

The clock on the crown of the Boustead Institute for Seamen showed ten o'clock when the police carriage dropped the detectives around the corner of the building. Hawksworth and Rizby slammed open the front door and strode in directly. They found Stewart standing at a desk on the ground floor, speaking with a clerk: Stewart blanched when he saw the Chief Detective Inspector.

'Why, Mr. Stewart, you look like you have seen a ghost!' Hawksworth said.

'I am surprised to see you here, Chief Detective Inspector,' the man sputtered.

'Why is that?'

'I thought you would have your hands full now, I mean with the Chinese clans.'

Hawksworth squared up to the man, his face only inches away from Stewart's. 'Where were you the night of 10 April?'

'I was in my office, here.'

'You were not. You were in the jungle with Mr. Chettiar. And his family.'

The blood drained from the man's face.

'Mr. Stewart, I request that you come with us to the Central Police Station to answer questions about your relationship with the Chettiars,' Hawksworth said.

The Scot quailed, but tried to stand his ground. 'I am a very busy man, Chief Detective Inspector. Is this absolutely necessary?'

'I am afraid so. If you do not want to come, then I will have to insist that you do.'

'On whose authority?'

'On the authority of the Straits Settlements Police—' Rizby began.

Hawksworth cut him short, barking in a hoarse voice, 'On the authority of Her Majesty Victoria, by the Grace of God, Monarch of the United Kingdom of Great Britain and Ireland, Defender of the Faith, and Empress of India, whose authority flows from Westminster across the vast seas and lands of her realm into this very body that now stands before you – and whom it has been my pleasure to serve since I was barely more than a boy. Now will you come with us to the station, Mr. Stewart, or will I have to shackle you and toss you into a bullock cart?'

Stewart whispered, 'Can we not do it in my office upstairs? Discretion is advised. He has men watching me.' He glanced around nervously, as though he were surrounded by invisible enemies.

Hawksworth studied the man for a second, and then looked at Rizby, whose fox-agate eyes never wavered from the Scot's face. He shrugged. 'Of course. I do not see the harm in that.'

Once in Stewart's office, they seated him roughly in one of the chairs, and each stood on either side of him. Hawksworth did not want him behind the desk, where he could open a drawer and pull out a weapon.

'How long have you known Mr. Chettiar?'

Stewart laughed, scoffing. 'My family and the Chettiar family have known each other ever since my grandfather served in the second Royal Scots regiment and borrowed money from Subramanian's grandfather. That was in 1815. We have done business with them ever since. I knew him before I ever set foot in Singapore. In fact, he was instrumental in securing for me this position at Boustead.' There was a nervous ring to his voice as he spoke, and this caught Hawksworth's attention. The man was hiding something.

'These Boustead and Company projects you intend to undertake on behalf of Mr. Chettiar – they are a cover operation of some sort, are they not? A way to transfer funds?'

'Of course not. We have every intention of opening the museum and temple.'

'So you can carry on with your sick debaucheries? I saw what you did to Chettiar's daughter. My god, she is only a child.'

Stewart laughed boldly. 'You are the child! When we are through with this, we will run you into the ground.' His expression changed suddenly, his mask of composure slipping to reveal a wild-eyed fanatic.

Hawksworth reacted instantly. 'You worm,' he grabbed the man's hair and jerked his head back hard. 'The only ones going into the ground around here are yourself and your fat friend. You will both be imprisoned for murder, arson, theft, and not to mention the perversity you practice.' He slammed the back of Stewart's head against the top of the chair.

Stewart was dazed but laughed malevolently, a maniac's gleam in his eyes. 'If we left it to you and your kind, the bloody Chinese would overrun us in no time. Families like the Lows will control Malaya, then Burma, and will then extend their tentacles all the way into India and subvert the Raj. What we are doing is saving the Empire from those backward yellow bastards.'

'Alastair Stewart, it is my duty to inform you that you are under arrest and will be held in confinement until your arraignment.' Hawksworth lowered his face to the man's ear: 'Next, we will catch your overblown playmate and make sure he pays for the crimes he has committed – most likely with his life.'

Stewart's eyes widened, and his face contorted hideously. He began to wail, 'You will never catch him! He is a great man, a *siddha*, a Perfected Being. He can control the natural world. When he heard that you came down to the plantation to find us, he used his power to make you ill. I thought he would kill you, but perhaps he took mercy on you. When he hears about what you have done to me, you shall truly suffer in agony.'

'I suppose,' Hawksworth turned to Rizby, remarking drily, 'you have some sort of amulet that will give me protection?'

'Oh, we knew about you but not about him,' Stewart pointed at Rizby. 'The old man we left to watch the house must have forgotten to tell us about him,' he started to snigger uncontrollably.

'The American?'

'A botched job,' he snorted gleefully. 'We paid him to bring the statue to us. The Kling crew was instructed to kill him as soon as it was safely delivered. They did follow orders, but then panicked and dumped the body in the Rochor Canal.'

'The ship that arrived from Batavia – it was carrying the statue, correct?'

'Yes. We sent it the long way round, in order to lead anyone who was pursuing it on a wild goose chase.' He was now rocking back and forth in his seat violently.

'The ship burning?'

'A fortuitous accident, perhaps. A tipped lantern or candle when a seaman was lighting joss sticks at the wharf's altar.'

'And what about poor Mr. Lamb?'

The snigger in his voice escalated into a deranged cackling that did not cease as he spoke, the veins in his forehead beginning to rise: 'His name was all too appropriate. We killed him and used his life-blood as our offering.'

'Where is the body?'

'We buried him in the very cemetery in which we mingled his essence with the essence of the Revered One. It is an *axis mundi*, a spiritual navel, a membrane between earth and hell. Your dear Lamb is in Yama's kingdom now.'

'Who dwells inside the statue?' Rizby asked in a low voice.

Stewart turned to him, his mouth curling into a vicious smile. His composure was now totally lost, his face twisting manically as he spoke, 'She is known as Bhuti, the Demoness of Dreams, the Waker of Desire, the Bringer of Nocturnal Emissions. She makes dreams come true but controls the dreams of those who do not know how to appease her. She makes visible the darkness that exists within all men.'

'The *tantra-mantra*?'

'We bring her forth with offerings of fresh human blood and our mixed sexual emissions. She inhabits the bodies of our women, and we mate with her through them to gain the power to control mortal men,' he was shouting. 'With her strength, we are unstoppable. We will rule not only Singapore but all of

Malaya. And then, India. Boustead and Company will rival the Raj in its power, and then we will rule over the Queen herself. Her dominions shall be ours!' Stewart's cackle flowed into hysterical laughter, then ebbed into gibbering as he leaped out of the chair with a monkey's primitive agility and started to chant, grinning, swaying, clawing at his clothes, trying to tear them off.

'*Kama-kama-kala-ha-im, kama-kama-kala-ha-im, kama-kama-kala-ha-im.*'

'Detective Inspector, restrain this man.'

Rizby remained immobile, mesmerised by the chanting man.

'Detective Inspector Rizby, your restraints, please!' Hawksworth barked. Rizby snapped to attention, pulling his shackles from his jacket. Hawksworth grabbed Stewart, who offered no resistance, and pinned his arms behind his back. Rizby clapped the shackles over his wrists. The man continued to chant softly to himself. Hawksworth slapped him so hard his nose began to bleed.

'Where is Chettiar now? And where is the statue?'

But Stewart said nothing, still swaying as if hypnotised, still chanting to himself, the horrible monkey grin fixed on his face, dark blood running from his nostril, dripping off his chin.

'To the station, sir?'

'To the asylum, Detective Inspector. We are taking this man to be warded.'

* * *

With Stewart's confession now secured, they could arrest Chettiar, but, predictably, the man was nowhere to be found. His house was empty and looked as if it had been prepared for a long absence, its furniture covered in sheets. His office staff said that he and his entire family were on holiday in India, but they had not been told exactly where. Hawksworth even checked at the icehouse, but the art works and artefacts were just as they had last left them there during their search.

'Perhaps he has left, sir,' Rizby said.

'I think not. His prize stallion is still stabled at the race track. One man could have helped us find him through the Kling underground, but Mohan is not in a position to talk to us anymore. I suppose that was also Chettiar's doing.'

'What should we do next, sir? We cannot arrest the horse, can we?'

'No, we cannot,' Hawksworth smiled at Rizby. 'I will check with my Chinese spies. Meanwhile, you turn your attention back to the clan war. We have wasted enough time on this madman and the missing statue for one day.'

The *kongsi* house on Almeida Street was shuttered, with ugly graffiti splashed across its front entrance, excrement piled in front of the door. Hawksworth knew he would have to find Yong Seng through other means.

* * *

That same night saw the first coolie uprising. It happened on a small plantation near Pasir Pajang. The Chinese coolies were convinced that the Kling overseer wanted to use them as sacrifice to appease an evil spirit he worshipped, the same entity that had been plaguing their dreams. About a dozen of them had decided to take action. The overseer was beaten then butchered. The coolies then surrounded the plantation house, torches burning, yelling and banging at the walls. The terrified family cowered inside while father and son loaded their weapons: a bird-gun and a revolver. Kicking open the front door, the son fired the bird-gun directly into the rabble, wounding one coolie and stripping the face off another. His father then stepped onto the veranda.

The coolies had been rendered silent and immobile, stunned by the first shots. It was then that the father shot the closest man point blank in his head. As he dropped, the next shot hit another coolie through the neck (the man would live). The remaining men ran helter-skelter for cover while the father calmly emptied his remaining four shots into their naked sweating backs, killing one and wounding two more. A dropped torch ignited a fire that quickly consumed a garden tool shed behind the main house.

The son had reloaded, but, as he told the constables when they showed up, the coolies had already run off. There was no one left to shoot.

They buried the poor Indian overseer the next day.

CHAPTER XIV

Changi Jetty

BY THE NEXT MORNING, the newspapers had turned the incident into a lurid tale of murderous rampage, near rape and bloody vengeance, praising the father and son who, while their house was burning to the ground, had supposedly fended off a deadly mob of nearly fifty Chinese hooligans. This was called the opening salvo in an all-out war between the *kongsi*, it was claimed, and the Chinese were not against inciting their loyal workers to rise against the British if it would give them an advantage. The European residents were advised to keep a sharp eye on their domestic helpers. If possible, their women and children should be sent abroad, immediately.

The Chinese quarter was dead silent. No shops were opened, no goods displayed on the five-foot-way, no hawkers calling out on the street. It was as if the entire population had vanished. They had not. They were hiding behind closed shutters, in locked rooms, waiting for rival clans to begin fighting on the streets, or for Sikh kill-squads to burst through doors, or for the big guns at Fort Canning to start booming. They too had heard of the uprising at Pasir Panjang, and they feared the worst. In their telling of the story, the family perished in the fire while the fatally wounded father – with one arm hacked off – still managed to kill dozens of attackers with a Maxim machine gun.

The army was mobilised to patrol the European districts and suburbs. Visitors were advised to bring their departure dates forward. A telegram was sent to London to apprise the Colonial Office of the situation and beg it to increase the garrison by sending men from Madras or Hong Kong.

It was rumoured that faced with the conjoined Hokkien clans, the Teochew-Cantonese factions were bringing reinforcements from the mainland – they were already on their way. Even worse, it was reported that cannons and mortars had been cast in Bangkok and were being smuggled into the colony; to which clan these were meant to be delivered, no one knew. It was said that Panglima Prang now resembled a fortress, the Low family digging in for a direct assault on their seat of power.

In two days, the announcement of the assignment of the spirit- and opium farms would appear in the newspapers. And then, everyone would brace for bloodshed that would make the rebellion of 1857 look like a circus sideshow in comparison. Meanwhile, the bodies of murdered and mutilated Chinese continued to stack up like cut sugarcane.

That morning Hawksworth found a young Chinese boy in blue pantaloons, his queue short like a girl's braid, waiting for him at the end of his front path. The boy held out a note, then scuffled off as quickly as his short legs would carry him. The message was from Yong Seng, and the Chief Detective Inspector was to rendezvous with him as soon as he got to town.

They met in a stuffy shophouse on Hokkien Street. Hawksworth noted that Yong Seng was dressed, like before, in his fine brocaded silks, his hair freshly washed and neatly parted, smelling of clove oil. An attendant poured gunpowder tea and served them steamed buns.

'You know where Chettiar is?'

'Yes. I also know something more.'

'Tell me.'

'I know that the Low family has heard of this statue, and that they now want it for themselves.'

'The Lows? Bloody hell! Whatever would they want to do with that thing?'

Yong Seng shrugged. 'They are strange. You have seen their house? Stuffed with junk.'

'You know Chettiar's whereabouts?'

'Yes. I have a man with him at all times now: his new Chinese valet is a Mother-Flower.' He added dispassionately, 'We had the previous one killed. A Cantonese.'

'Yong Seng, I do not need to know these things.' Hawksworth said bluntly. 'Where is Chettiar now? Is the statue with him?'

'No, it is not. But he is planning to leave Singapore, on a ship from the jetty at Changi. He is fleeing with the statue to Johor, where his family is already waiting for him.'

'We should arrest him now.'

'The statue is not with him, though. We assume that he will have it with him on the boat.'

'When does he leave?'

'Tonight. But I do not yet know the time.'

'And the Lows are demanding this statue?'

'We are meeting with their *samseng ong* – Low's own son – in one hour to discuss the trade. And a truce.'

'Of course. I did not think you had dressed so nicely to have tea with me.'

Yong Seng laughed the high Chinese laugh that meant true humour. 'But I do have something for you. That is for later though. For now we need to discuss our plan.'

'We stop Chettiar at the jetty, arrest him and recover the statue.'

'And if the statue is … lost?'

'You mean, if instead of returning the statue to the Maharaja of Mysore we turn it over to the Lows?'

He nodded affirmatively.

'Is that a condition of your truce with the Lows?'

He nodded again. Hawksworth brooded for a moment, and then said, 'I will have to use the statue as evidence for this investigation. They can have it afterward.'

This time the nod was negative. 'No, we must hand it over to the Lows now. A new alliance will be born from this, and together we will push out the Hai San.'

'I cannot allow that.'

'I could have simply killed him and taken the thing, but it is out of respect for our friendship that I give this man to you. If you want to arrest Chettiar, I will send word to you as soon as I know what time he will depart, and you can catch him at Changi jetty. However, Chief Detective Inspector, we will be there too. You will arrest Chettiar, and we will take the statue. You have been warned by Chong Yong Chern himself: do not interfere with our plans with the Lows.'

For the first time since they have been friends, Yong Seng had used a threatening tone with him. Hawksworth simply nodded in agreement. He sipped the last of his tea and the two men rose to depart, but Yong Seng said, 'Wait. I said I had a surprise for you.'

He clapped once and a side door opened. Shu En burst out into the light. She leapt to Hawksworth and flung her arms around him in a tight hug, burrowing her head into his belly. Hawksworth was too taken aback to speak. Yong Seng snorted the light Chinese snort that meant mild derision at life's foibles, and then said, 'I must go now. You take your time. And remember, Hawksworth, I will see you tonight at Changi jetty. We have a deal.'

He was gone before Hawksworth could get a sense of the situation. His heart pounding, he clasped her closely and gazed down into her moonglow face, her pink coral lips, her lanceolate gypsy eyes, her jet black hair. She said 'hello' in heavily accented English. She looked and felt nothing like the evil presence that had haunted his dreams for the past weeks.

He slid one hand down her back. She wore a light cotton smock, and he could feel her smooth skin beneath his fingertips, soft and naked. He tilted her chin upward to him. She was smiling in happy surrender. 'You are a stainless lotus of light,' he whispered, and then brought his lips to hers, his fingers caressing her smooth cheek and thin neck, drinking in her lychee scent.

'Destroy the bloody thing! Burn it or melt it or explode it!' The
veins in Walker's neck were bulging.

'To destroy it might release whatever is trapped inside,' Rizby
disagreed.

They were in Hawksworth's office, planning their actions
for that evening. Sergeant Major Walker had agreed to provide
additional fire power with his Martini-Henry rifle.

Walker chortled dismissively. 'There is nothing inside the
bloody statue, Detective Inspector. A hunk of metal is all it is.
Nothing more.'

'It is more than that. It is a reservoir of dreams in which
resides—'

'It is disturbing the order in Singapore and needs to be
removed. I say we dispose of it and the fat Kling at the same time.
Send them both to the bottom of Johor Strait.'

'Enough!' Hawksworth barked. 'We are to apprehend those
responsible for stealing the thing and then return it to its rightful
owner. That is the task we have been charged with, and that is
exactly what we shall do. We will arrest Subramanian Chettiar.
He will then be arraigned, tried and executed according to the
law. Then we close this case.' He did not mention to even his most
trusted troops about the deal that the Mother-Flower clan had
made with the Lows, or about the deal that he had made with the
Mother-Flowers.

'It is nearly half past five already. Where is this Chinese friend
of yours? How will he contact you when it is dangerous for him

even to walk the streets?'

'He will contact me. We should be ready at a moment's notice. Detective Inspector, collect our men. Sergeant Major Walker, prepare your Martini-Henry,' Hawksworth said definitively.

'Aye. And both my Webleys.'

Rizby addressed Hawksworth, 'Should I instruct the men to bring their weapons?'

'I want every man armed for war. Take revolvers from the armoury. But do it discretely.'

'What are you going to bring?' Walker wanted to know, a vicious gleam in his eye.

'My truncheon and my shackles, Sergeant Major,' Hawksworth said resolutely. 'I will bring my truncheon and my shackles.'

* * *

There was a knock at his door. A uniformed constable entered, 'Excuse me, Chief Detective Inspector, there is a telephone call for you.'

'Telephone? What a bother,' Hawksworth sighed in exasperation before resigning himself to the circumstances. He followed the constable down the main stairs to the telephone room. Another constable held the ear piece out to him. The tall man had to stoop uncomfortably to speak into the bell, his forehead resting on the telephone's wooden box. 'Hello?' he said uncertainly, then thought to identify himself, 'This is Chief Detective Inspector Hawksworth.'

He was surprised to hear Yong Seng's voice, thin and brassy on the line. 'Seven-thirty, Changi jetty. The ship's captain is our man. Arrest Chettiar. We will take the boat and statue. Remember, Chief Detective Inspector, do not interfere with our plans.'

The line went dead. Fuzzy static buzzed in Hawksworth's ear. 'How did Yong Seng gain access to a telephone?' he wondered aloud as he glanced at his pocket watch. It was already quarter to seven.

* * *

The horse and carriage raced at top speed, Iqbal sitting with the driver, Anaiz, Rizby, Walker and Hawksworth inside. Walker was stroking the polished wood stock of his rifle. Coming off the main road, they took progressively narrower roads until they were on a dirt track running through coastal shrub.

They stopped the carriage before the sound of the horse hooves would alert anyone of their presence and crept through the overgrowth, making their way to the short wooden jetty that protruded from the beach. They could make out at the far end of the structure a two-masted black tongkang, a green-sea serpent painted on the prow, wicked red eyes peering outward.

'There must be two dozen of them,' Iqbal said. 'We are outnumbered!'

The jetty was filled with Kling men. Some were loading the ship, some preparing to board it, others standing guard on the landward side; almost all of them were armed with swords and staffs, at least two had rifles.

'Far more than I had expected,' Hawksworth murmured, wondering where the Mother-Flowers could be hiding themselves. He would need reinforcements.

'There are only eighteen of them. I have counted,' Walker said, unholstering his Webley revolvers. 'Ready?'

Before anyone had time to answer, he exploded from the foliage, a pistol in each fist. He aimed first for the men with the rifles, both his weapons firing in turn, and then began to fire randomly into the other men. The big .455 slugs tore apart the bodies they hit, spattering blood. At least five men went down; the two with the rifles were shredded.

As soon as Walker's pistols fell silent, Hawksworth's men sprang from behind him. Anaiz and Iqbal opened fire with the .32 police revolvers, taking aim at men with visible weapons. A few more Klings dropped to the ground, wounded or dead.

The jetty was now in tumult as men sought shelter from the policemen's spray of bullets. Some leaped onto the ship only to be tossed back by those already on board. Others jumped into the sea. When the firing had stopped, the two groups squared off across the open ground that lay between the end of the jetty and Hawksworth's line.

Walker drew a foot-long bayonet from a scabbard on his belt and charged while Anaiz and Iqbal took his flanks, one with his truncheon, the other with his short-bladed kris. They met the enemy with full force. As the two groups merged, slashing gave way to stabbing, which then gave way to punching and kicking. A melee ensued.

While the three men grappled with a force two-to-one on their own, Hawksworth and Rizby ran for the jetty to try to catch the boat before it could cast off. Hawksworth heard a bullet whistle past his head, another cracked overhead. Both he and Rizby ducked and rolled for cover behind the thick timber pilings that anchored the jetty to the shore. Chunks of wood flew as two more rounds flew towards them, slamming into the timber, splintering the piling and shaking the jetty.

'Good god, what is that? An elephant gun?' Hawksworth shouted.

The rifle boomed again from the ship, blowing a hunk out of the top of the piling he was crouching behind. Rizby lifted his Tranter .32 calibre revolver and began to return fire. It silenced the rifle intermittently, but otherwise the small-calibre rounds did little from the far end of the jetty, merely plunking into the hull of the ship.

'We need to get down there before they cast off. Reload and provide cover. I will run for it,' Hawksworth yelled, unhooking his truncheon. Another round pounded into the post Rizby was covering behind, sending splinters flying. He ignored it and began refilling his cylinder.

Hawksworth looked back to see Iqbal rolling on the ground, a Kling of equal size on top of him. Blood was pouring from the detective's temple. Walker loomed up and yanked the Kling off the detective, then stuck his bayonet into the man's chest. He let the man drop and pulled Iqbal up. The two then stood back to back, ready for the next attacker.

'This is my final cylinder. You have got to get there now!' Rizby shouted.

It was more than forty yards to the tongkang. Rizby leaned over and started shooting. Hawksworth was rising to dash when a foot landed in his side, knocking him over. He rolled and sprang into a defensive crouch, his truncheon held ready to strike.

A tall Kling with ropey muscles came at him, a *kattari* gripped in each fist, the short double-edged blades protruding from the man's knuckles, the knife's tangs running down either side of his wrist.

Hawksworth rose and deflected the Kling's first blow with his truncheon, but a blade came in quickly from below and slashed his belly, cutting him deeply. Hawksworth stepped back, but the Kling twisted with the momentum of Hawksworth's deflection and brought down his other blade. Instinctively, Hawksworth ducked then rolled to his left, onto the ground. He struck his truncheon behind the Kling's left knee and popped out the leg from under the man. The Kling stumbled but kept his balance by pivoting the other way on his right foot. As Hawksworth scrambled upward, several bones in his foot snapped painfully out of place, for it had not mended fully since the explosion, and he gritted his teeth as his truncheon slipped from his hand.

The Kling quickly closed the ground. The Chief Detective Inspector balanced defenceless on one leg, ready to bring his bare fists into play against the mad flashing blades of the deadly *kattaris*.

Then, abruptly, the assailant was lifted away. Hawksworth looked up into the face of Cheang Sam Teo, the orang-utan–sized man from the Mother-Flower *kongsi*, who hoisted the flailing Kling above his head, then snapped him once before flinging him through the air. The body landed with a dull thud, then lay still.

Grunting, the orang-utan then rushed to the Kling who was facing off with Anaiz. He scooped up the man, pinning him against his own body. Anaiz plunged his kris between the Kling's ribs and sawed the wavy blade back and forth, plunging it into the lungs, and then the heart. Blood gurgled from the dead man's mouth as Teo let him slip to the ground.

Behind him, five more of Yong Seng's men were grappling with the remaining Klings; one held in his hands the long, curved blade of a scimitar. Yong Seng himself ran up to Hawksworth and steadied his friend. 'Not a moment too soon, my brother.'

'We wanted to give the fat one time to board his ship,' he said, and Hawksworth turned to see that the tongkang had cast off, its foresail already unfurled. The ship was sailing away.

He saw Rizby standing at the end of the jetty, his arms dropped limply by his sides, the Tranter still held in one hand, the revolver smoking but empty. Beyond him, Chettiar's head could be seen peeking above the gunwale of the stern, watching the situation on shore.

'Hell's bells! We cannot have that man leave!' Hawksworth ran hobbling towards Walker, who was reloading his Webleys. 'Sergeant Major, your rifle!'

Walker glanced up and saw that the tongkang was under sail. He dropped his pistols, unslung his rifle and quickly chambered a round. He shouldered the weapon just as Chettiar's head peaked out again. Seeing the distance he had managed to put between him and the detectives, and believing himself to be safe now, Chettiar waved tauntingly to the men on the receding shore.

'Shoot him,' Hawksworth barked.

The ship was at least a hundred and fifty yards away from where they stood on dry land. Walker adjusted the sliding back sight, keeping a bead on Chettiar's fat grinning face.

There was a sharp report from the Martini-Henry, followed by a surreal moment of prolonged stillness, as though the air had grown as thick as water, while the .577 lead bullet travelled over warm land and cool sea towards the head of the man on the aft deck of the gently rolling ship.

Chettiar's skull exploded, his blood and brain matter splattering on the mizzen-mast behind him. As his body crumpled then collapsed behind the gunwale, the waving arm remained comically erect, frozen in his final gesture, as if he were waving goodbye to the living world.

Hawksworth blew a long exhalation. 'Bloody impressive shot, Sergeant Major.'

'Black bastard,' Walker glowered as he lowered the rifle from his shoulder, working the lever to eject the smoking brass.

The five policemen watched helplessly as the black-hulled ship sailed across the straits, the setting sun momentarily colouring the sea deep burgundy. The cries of the wounded brought them back, suddenly, to the action of the moment. The land around them was littered with Kling bodies, and Yong Seng and his *kongsi* men seemed to have vanished into the air, leaving the detectives to the malodorous process task of sorting the living from the dead.

CHAPTER XV

Hungry Ghosts

It was late dusk, the road only dimly visible from the veranda of Hawksworth's bungalow, where he and Ni sat beside a single lamp, eating fresh jackfruit after dinner. His glass was on the rattan table beside them, sweating. After his illness, the Chief Detective Inspector had discovered a liking for sweet arrack distilled from coconut flowers. He mixed the amber drink with fresh lime juice and ice, for he had also developed an affinity for 'stone water' in his drinks. He and Ni now had a bulky ice box in their bungalow's kitchen. They had also arranged for weekly deliveries from the Singapore Ice Company.

Hawksworth went in to chip more ice for his arrack, preoccupied with his thoughts about the Chettiar case. His foot still throbbed from time to time, especially during the change in monsoons. An official inquiry had determined that the explosion at the Central Police Station had been accidental: a constable had dropped a box of cartridges and managed to set off the entire crate. It was believed that gunpowder had spilled from some of the brass, and this had resulted in the massive detonation. Whatever the cause, Hawksworth still walked with a slight limp.

Young Mr. Welbore had eventually recovered from his fever, having been ill throughout the investigation and looming *kongsi* war, only to return to the India Office empty-handed. The statue was never recovered, and, it was officially reported, was believed lost at sea.

Chettiar's body was found sloshing around the beach at Bedok two days after he had been shot. When they found him, he was literally empty-headed: the fish had made a feast of what little brain matter had remained inside his skull.

The much-feared open warfare between the *kongsi* had never materialised. The opium and spirit farm assignments were announced, and as the European town had braced for a siege, the Chinese quarter had sprung back into life and resumed business as though nothing had ever been amiss. The head-cutting scare was quickly forgotten, and life in the colony, as far as the Europeans were concerned, continued much as before.

Hawksworth did hear that key clan alliances had shifted, with the Lows now aligned with the Mother-Flowers, although the Hai San still controlled the opium farm. He did not see Chong Yong Chern as often as before. He was now the head of a much larger operation, for the Mother-Flower *kongsi* had amalgamated several other Hokkien groups, and was a very busy man. Yong Seng and he would still meet to drink and talk from time to time. He had confided in Hawksworth that Shu En had Yong Chern completely wrapped around her little finger and could be seen sitting by his side during *kongsi* meetings. It was rumoured, Yong Seng said, that the most powerful Hokkien clan was really being run by the former *mui tsai* girl.

Hawksworth poured the lime juice into his arrack, then dipped his finger in to stir. He had never asked Yong Seng about the fate or whereabouts of the statue; Hawksworth had thought it prudent not to press the man about it.

Alastair Stewart had been sent under lock and key to London. He was found to be insane and was now a patient in one of the larger mental hospitals, where he told stories of a flying demoness and of world conquest to anyone who would listen to him.

When Hawksworth returned to the veranda, the ice tinkling pleasantly in his glass, Gazali, the *bomoh* from the neighbouring kampong, was standing at the top of the steps with a respectful smile.

'*Selamat malam*, tuan.'

'*Malam*, Gazali. How is life keeping you?'

'Very well, tuan, very well. Today I delivered not one but two children into this blessed world. Allah willing, they will grow to be big and strong.'

'Allah willing, they shall. What can I do for you?'

'I was passing by and saw that many people have left offerings by the roadside. I wanted to ask if you, too, have left offerings?'

It was the seventh lunar month, the month of Hungry Ghosts, when the gates of hell opened and the deceased walked the earth. They needed appeasement, and hell money was burnt, joss sticks lit, and food left to rot before shrines. For the Chinese, this was a festival of music and drinking, and the boisterous entertainments they put on at night were as much fun for the living as they were for the dead: the front rows at the caterwauling operas and portable puppet plays were always left empty for the spirits to have the best seats.

The traffic around the banyan tree was particularly heavy during this time. All day long and into the night, a procession of people, not only Chinese but all types and from all around the nearby kampongs, arrived there to light joss sticks and candles, to kneel and pray to the spirit that dwelt in the old tree.

Hawksworth was puzzled by the *bomoh*'s question. 'No, I did not. Why do you ask?'

Gazali cast an eye at Ni, and then said in a lower tone. 'I told you before about the black lady who came to me in my dreams?'

Hawksworth nodded. 'Yes, has she gone?'

'She has! Many months ago the dreams stopped. But last night I had a dream about you. I believe that you may be in danger, tuan. Because you are a good man, I wanted to warn you.'

'What kind of danger, Gazali?'

'Tuan, I cannot say. Dreams are not specific. But I advise you not to undertake any travel for some time. Some little demons are angry with you for some reason. Have you offended them?'

'Really, Gazali, I am in no danger, I assure you.'

Gazali pressed the palms of his hands together and kissed the top of his fingertips. He then extended his right palm forward and placed it over Hawksworth's chest, above his heart, and murmured some words. This done, he smiled at Hawksworth and said, 'Good night, tuan. Many happy days lie ahead for you. And for her,' and he smiled at Ni before heading towards the dark road, past the banyan tree, where small candles flickered, attracting fluttering moths.

Not long after, Hawksworth and Ni were just about to head

inside for the night when a uniformed constable, hardly more than a boy, came running up the path. 'Chief Detective Inspector! Chief Detective Inspector!' He sprinted up the steps, panting, and held out a sealed letter to the tall man.

'Easy, constable, easy. What is your name?'

'I am Joseph Jeremiah, sir. I have just joined the force. I have come all the way, sir, from Central Station on foot to deliver this letter to you.'

'Good lord, what is it?' he asked, tearing into the envelope.

'It is from Sergeant Major Walker, sir.' He knew that several weeks earlier, Walker had headed a force to the town of Muar in Johor, between Malacca and Gunung Ledang, the mountain the British called Mount Ophir.

'It arrived by today's post. He has instructed that it be delivered to you urgently, unopened.'

Hawksworth held the Sergeant's note close to the lamp and read it quickly. He then stood, pale as a sheet, looking as though he were about to faint. Ni grabbed his arm in concern. 'What does it say, sir?' Jeremiah asked.

'As Sergeant Major Walker was passing through Malacca after his force disembarked, he dined with the local constabulary. He says he met an elderly woman named Lim Suan Imm. As they were discussing Singapore, my name came up. She told him that she knows of me. She claims to have known my parents. And ...' he struggled to go on. Ni clung more tightly to his arm. He looked into her concerned face, smoothing back her hair. 'I must travel first thing in the morning. This Suan Imm believes that my mother is still alive. And that she is in grave danger.'

Historical Note

I have made every effort to be as accurate and as true as possible to the historical conditions of the early 1890s while still writing a contemporary novel. I have tried to avoid putting anachronisms into the mouths of nineteenth-century characters, but some may have slipped through. The titles of British colonial figures have been slightly modernised for ease of reading. Although many of the family names in the book will be familiar to modern Singaporeans, every character in the book, except for specific historical figures, is totally fictitious.

Whenever possible, I have used the street names as they appeared during the period. Almeida Street, for instance, became Temple Street only in 1909, and Japan Street became Boon Tat Street after the Second World War.

Many of the buildings described in the book existed. Panglima Prang was built by Tan Jiak Kim in the late 1850s. It was the oldest private house in Singapore when it was demolished in 1982 to make way for condominiums. An explosion in the forecourt of the Central Police Station occurred in 1891; a clock tower, visible in many old photos, was erected during repairs. The Station was completed in 1886 and demolished in 1977. A modern office building currently stands on the site. Outram Prison was constructed in 1882 and demolished in 1970 to make room for government housing; this was, in turn, demolished roughly thirty years later. Currently the land is open park space. The Boustead Institute for Seaman was constructed in 1892 and demolished in 1976; the X-shaped junction on which it stood was obliterated in the early 1980s to make room for the modern Tanjong Pagar container port. The icehouse was built in 1854 by Hoo Ah Kay, also known as 'Whampoa'. It was demolished in 1981. The site is now home to the G-max Reverse Bungy attraction, part of the Clarke Quay food and entertainment complex. As of this writing, the icehouse at Madras still stands.

The Chinese 'secret societies' of Southeast Asia are known by a number of names in the historical sources: *hoeys* (an Anglicisation of 'Hui') or associations; *pangs* or guilds; clans, triads, and finally *kongsi*. I have used '*kongsi*' and 'clan' and 'gang' throughout the book for means of narrative expediency and for no other reason. Some of these societies were based on family, village or dialect affiliations, while others were centred on particular temple, business or labour groups. Their nature ranged from what we would today think of as cooperative associations to religious organisations, and even to fearsome Mafia-style crime syndicates. While some of these groups maintained a low profile, they were only 'secret' in so much that most of them required some sort of ritual bonding of their members and the conducting of some observances that were kept deliberately cryptic. In this they were – indeed still are – no more or less 'secret' than a Western fraternal organisation like the Masons. The colonial authorities eventually came to distrust the Chinese societies not only because they were often affiliated with nefarious activities but also because in their organisation and control of both people and economies, they represented an alternative form of governance.

This book is not only fiction but fantasy, and I have played somewhat fast and loose with Hindu cosmology while trying to adhere to actual ritual practice and symbolism as much as possible.

What many people in the West believe they are doing when they engage in the tame New Age version of 'Tantric sex' is very far from the practice as it originated in India. The Tantric cult rituals often required orgies in cremation grounds that involved 'unnatural' sex acts such as oral and anal couplings and the drinking of mixed bodily fluids. The rituals were meant to summon female demons known as *Yoginis*. It was believed that the *Yoginis* would incarnate themselves within female worshipers in order to have sex with the men, resulting in the granting of supernatural powers such as flight and immortality. For detailed information on this subject, see David Gordon White's *Kiss of the Yogini: 'Tantric Sex' in its South Asian Contexts.*

More by William L. Gibson

Singapore Yellow

Singapore/Malaya, 1892: Chief Detective Inspector David Hawksworth, orphaned, middle-aged and gimlet-eyed, travels to Malacca to meet a mysterious woman who claims his mother is alive, only to find a British Resident has been brutally murdered and a Singapore police expedition has vanished in the jungle. Children are being snatched from villages, sinister commercial syndicates are fighting over virgin resources, and a seductive vampiric *pontianak* is on the loose. When native kids start turning up butchered in Singapore, Hawksworth finds himself increasingly isolated as the evidence points to the involvement of the colonial elite. Bringing justice to the powerful perpetrators while saving his own skin and uncovering the secrets of his dark past pushes the detective over the brink in this thrilling sequel to *Singapore Black.*

Singapore Red

Singapore/Malaya, 1895: A cholera epidemic breaks out in Singapore's congested Chinatown, and Detective Inspector Hawksworth finds himself embroiled in a case that threatens to spill over into regional warfare. While the immigrant population threatens to riot, someone is smuggling powerful new American weapons into the British colony, and rumours of Chinese undead wandering the night-time streets puts even the powerful Chinese clans on edge.